THE BRASS RING

THE BRASS RING

Kay Stephens

Thorndike Press • Chivers Press
Thorndike, Maine USA   Bath, England

This Large Print edition is published by Thorndike Press, USA and by Chivers Press, England.

Published in 1999 in the U.S. by arrangement with Chivers Press Ltd.

Published in 1999 in the U.K. by arrangement with Severn House Publishers Ltd.

U.S. Hardcover 0-7862-2086-4 (Romance Series Edition)
U.K. Hardcover 0-7540-1335-9 (Windsor Large Print)
U.K. Softcover 0-7540-2249-8 (Paragon Large Print)

The text of this Large Print edition is unabridged. Other aspects of the book may vary from the original edition.

Set in 16 pt. Plantin by Minnie B. Raven.

Printed in the United States on permanent paper.

British Library Cataloguing-in-Publication Data available

Library of Congress Cataloging-in-Publication Data

Stephens, Kay
    The brass ring / Kay Stephens.
      p. cm.
    ISBN 0-7862-2086-4 (lg. print : hc : alk. paper)
    1. Large type books. I. Title.
    [PR6069.T4293B73 1999]
    823'.914—dc21   99-33352

For my husband, with love.

CHAPTER ONE

'I do not approve, Georgina; you must see that I cannot.'

Even as he assisted her from the carriage, Roland was still trying to dissuade her.

She drew in a deep breath and met the chill gaze of his grey eyes.

'This is something I have always longed to do. Always.'

He sighed. 'Once, you talked of nothing but marrying me . . .'

'And I *will*,' Georgina interrupted, 'truly, Roland, I will. But first I must prove that I can do this work.'

'Work!' His full face reddened with indignation. 'Your task should be as mistress of my home.'

'But . . .'

'Let me finish. And if you fear you would have insufficient to occupy your time, you could keep your mama company when your father's away fighting Bonaparte.'

'You know I am an artist, that I have trained . . .'

'My dear,' he said, 'I would allow you time

for drawing pictures.'

Georgina withdrew her fingers from her fiancé's grasp and turned towards the house in Grosvenor Place.

Roland watched her walking from him and saw the shoulders straightening, the slender neck stretching to support a dark head whose angle expressed determination. Already, she seemed taller than her medium height, scarcely familiar. If he had loved her less he would have loathed this implied independence sufficiently to ride back to Sevenoaks without her.

Instead, he would wait until Georgina emerged, for then she would need his support in what, he felt certain, would be her rejection. Dear, foolish, girl — neither reason nor good sense could prevail upon her.

One day she would appreciate his stability. Although the concern he'd shown during her development into a spirited eighteen-year-old had caused a deal of dissension.

At the door, Georgina paused before ringing the bell, and withdrew from her glove the printed pasteboard that was her introduction. Her fingers trembled and she willed them to be still, nothing must betray her nervousness. She had done as she thought best and would need all her self-possession now to secure the position.

The arch, aproned female who admitted her gave the card a cursory glance, blinked, and then scrutinized the words as though they were foreign.

'I have an appointment with Mr Saunders,' Georgina stated, 'would you please tell him that I am here.'

The woman nodded her muslin cap, but assent could not have been further from her expression and she narrowed thin nostrils before striding towards the rear of the house.

Georgina could hear the woman's voice, rising in astonishment, as she spoke with her master.

The starched collar seemed to crackle its own disapproval as the woman returned along the hall. The thin throat shuddered when she swallowed before speaking, as though she could hardly bring herself to act on Georgina's behalf.

'Would you come this way, please . . .'

The man sitting at the mahogany desk was slender in appearance so that the blue eyes came as a shock; their strength was challenging.

'One moment . . .' He waved a hand towards a chair and looked back to the papers on the desk.

Georgina seated herself on the straight-backed chair and gazed approvingly towards the ornate plasterwork ceiling. Her glance continued to wood-panelled walls, relieved only by bookshelves and the windows whose patterned curtaining was of a complexity identifying its source as a Jacquard loom.

'I assume that Mr Morton was unable to be present himself and has sent you in his place,' Howard Saunders began, at last, still preoccupied with his paperwork. 'I would have appreciated the courtesy of an explanation. I could then have explained, in turn, that I do not conduct my professional affairs with messengers.'

'But I am not,' Georgina protested, then found words eluding her as he allowed her again the full power of his deep blue gaze.

She gulped, and was furious with her emotions betraying her.

'You are . . . whom . . . George Morton's daughter perhaps?'

'No, I . . .'

'His sister then?'

'No. No, I am no relation.'

'Then who are you — and why have you used this card to gain admittance here when my appointment with him clearly . . . ?'

Georgina interrupted. 'I am afraid you have become a little confused, Mr Saunders.

You see, that is my calling card, just as the name it bears is that with which I sign all my work.'

'I beg your pardon?'

'I am the artist whose signature is Geo. Morton . . .'

'You are *whom?*' The roar from her host was so loud that it belied his slight build, and when he sprang to his feet he appeared so tall that she felt she was surveying the top of a poplar tree.

'I am Georg— Georgina Morton.'

'The devil you are! And devilish cunning in the tricks you employ!'

'Tricks?'

He flipped the card across the desk towards her. 'Masquerading as a man to gain my notice. If you sought amusement I trust you are satisfied, for I am not. I *work,* madam, and waste no time over frivolities!'

'Frivolities?'

He turned and strode towards the bell-pull. 'You will forgive me, I am sure, if I do not escort you personally to the door. As I have said, I am . . .'

'. . . too busy to give me a fair hearing.'

He had started at the word fair, the silken bell-pull slithered from long fingers as he faced her. A quizzical blond eyebrow invited explanation.

'I understood from Professor Anstey that James MacInnes had died and you were in need of an artist to finish illustrating the guide to Scotland that you are writing.'

'And if that were so, what then? I'll have much to warm the ears of our professional friend when next we meet. Sending me a bit of a girl, indeed . . . !'

Georgina inhaled sharply, took out a letter, and continued. 'I understand also, from yourself, that you found the samples of my work "extremely fine", and you expected that I should be "more than adequate to continuing the task commenced by Mr MacInnes".' She had no need of his letter as reminder, for his words had become etched into her life.

Howard Saunders was gazing at her, amazed. Now the initial shock was abating and he'd really looked at this creature, he was finding concentration difficult. The brown direct eyes held such appeal a cooler man than he would have struggled to remain unmoved. And the hair — those dark tendrils tumbling about the piquant face from around a glossy chignon — enticed him to touch. Or, more circumspectly, to describe. Yet well he knew even *his* pen would be sorely taxed to find terms that would do justice to the attractiveness, enhanced by a high-waisted gown in golden silk with its matching pelisse.

'Since you've changed your mind about my work, I will take my portfolio of drawings with me.'

Blundering against a corner of the desk, he went to get the folder.

Her generous pink lips were compressed into a thin line, as she extended a hand. Suddenly, he felt reluctant to have her blame him for the failure of her mission.

'Professor Anstey should have told me,' he said, 'then there would have been no misunderstanding.'

Georgina shrugged resignedly. 'He warned me that you could well be displeased, but from your letter I'd believed you would not be prejudiced.'

'Prejudiced?'

Her beautiful lips curved, but their smile was wry. 'Oh, please . . . do not add hypocrisy to the rest.'

She had grasped the folder of drawings, but instead of releasing his hold he drew a little closer to her.

'No — wait,' he said.

Georgina scarcely understood the simple words. Her vision wavered as she trembled, and even as she wondered if disappointment were making her faint she realized that this man's proximity alone was causing her unease. Reason cautioned her to move away, yet excitement coursed through her veins to hold her as though by some magnet.

'Perhaps you would sit down once more . . .'

She nodded, backing away from him to a chair; sitting was precisely what her unstable legs demanded.

'I see that I have disturbed you.'

Startled, Georgina frowned. That she had experienced this — this fluttering sensation were bad enough, but to have him guess . . .!

'I am sorry if I have upset you, but you must understand that had I known Geo. Morton was a young lady I couldn't have entertained the possibility of your working with me.'

Relief that he had recognized only one cause of her agitation liberated her tongue. 'You have made that plain already, and my time also has some value.'

He sighed. 'There are reasons, and good ones at that, why a girl does not accept such a position.'

'Oh, yes, indeed!' She sprang to her feet. 'Because men like you want to believe you're the only ones capable. While we — we are supposed to content ourselves with needlework, playing the piano — or sipping tea. Or maybe, if we are so inclined, with becoming a governess or paid companion . . .'

Devoid of breath, she paused. His blue eyes were smiling, though the firm lips seemed disciplined against humour.

'Well, I am *not* so inclined, Mr Saunders; one day you will learn that I am an illustrator.'

'But not of topographical books.'

'It's what I do well, even you admitted that.'

Somehow, he had retained her portfolio. She motioned him to hand it to her, and then she stalked towards the door. He was there before her, his hand on its carved knob.

'A second more,' he insisted. 'I would ask simply that you now contemplate — as you evidently have not — the hazards that would face a young lady travelling in this country and elsewhere.'

Puzzled, she glanced up at him.

'There are those who waylay a coach, seeking to rob its passengers, or worse.'

'Surely all roads are safer now, since the introduction of Horse Patrols?'

'They have eased matters. But they protect London chiefly. You cannot imagine the dangers beyond . . .'

Georgina smiled. 'Mr Saunders, I am not

quite the sheltered imbecile that you think me. I have read widely — some volumes which you yourself have written to encourage such interest. And I have talked with those who are familiar with the roads, even beyond my native Kent. I remain determined to explore them.'

'Yes, but . . .'

'Furthermore, my father serves with Wellesley's army, and although he has raised no sons, none of his offspring is lacking in mettle.' Her eyes glinted with amusement.

His laugh was as sharp as it was unexpected. When his hand went to her arm she wished his fingers elsewhere because of the effect they were having.

'I must go,' she announced. 'For you will not even let me try . . .'

'How can I?' he interrupted, 'how — when by so doing I would place your life and . . .' He swallowed hard, his gaze in its candid appraisal of her bosom, barely concealed by gold silk, revealing his other fears for her. '. . . at risk,' he concluded.

'I would not hold you responsible for my well-being,' she assured him. 'But I know you are varnishing over the fact that you don't wish me to work with you. My one regret now is that you were less than honest.'

His pale complexion flared and Georgina

disciplined a satisfied smile. She had intended to rouse Howard Saunders.

She stared at the hand still reposing on her arm. 'If you please, Mr Saunders. I am leaving . . .'

Somehow, he slipped his lean body between Georgina and the door. Unable to remain standing only inches from him, she stepped back.

'Less than honest am I?' he demanded. 'I can see how you have arrived at this conclusion. We'll waste no more time wrangling over what a young lady should or should not do. Very well, Miss Morton, you shall have your opportunity. I leave for Scotland in one week's time. You will accompany me.'

Georgina quelled a gasp to smile. 'Thank you. I — I will ensure that you're not disappointed with my work.'

'We shall see.'

'As I mentioned in my letters, I am familiar with several engraving methods and am accustomed to preparing my own copper plates.'

'There'll be no necessity for that. MacInnes was an artist, and it is simply an artist that I require. I have an excellent engraver.'

'Very well.'

'Do not sound deflated, Miss Morton.

17

You'll have plenty to tax your craftsman-ship. My book is completed all but the illus-trations, you'll have to work swiftly to win my approval.'

'I will do my best.'

'You'll do well to remember that should you fail you will be on the first mail coach for your home.'

He stepped away from the door just as an elegant woman walked quickly into the room.

Almost as tall as Howard Saunders, she had an assured bearing that emphasized the impact of her exquisitely proportioned figure and beautiful features. Her red hair was perfectly coiffured and the green eyes seemed to dare anyone to find the minutest fault with her.

'Forgive me,' she addressed Mr Saunders, 'I believed you were alone.'

Georgina had noticed that his gaze had been drawn instantly to this lovely woman, whose fashionable gown of green satin had the lowest décolletage that she had ever seen.

'No matter,' he murmured. 'May I present Miss Georgina Morton who will be working for me on my book. Miss Morton, I would like to introduce Lady Virginia Mayburn.'

The hand that accepted Georgina's was icy, its pressure slight. In place of any exchange of pleasantries Lady Virginia turned to Howard Saunders.

'Working on your book?'

'Miss Morton is an artist.'

'Indeed?' Lady Virginia Mayburn treated Georgina to a look brief enough to imply that she might be dismissed.

'Was there something you required, Virginia?' Mr Saunders asked.

'Later, my dear, later,' she said, and glided from the room.

'I think we should finalize our arrangements for our visit to Scotland,' Mr Saunders said when Georgina remained staring rather dazedly towards the door.

'Of course.'

On his desk was a map that she'd noticed earlier. 'May I?' she reached over and turned it around. 'I was wondering about the maps you would be using in your book. I have some experience of cartography . . .'

She got no further. His hand slapped down on top of her own, stinging the flesh with the impact.

'If you please, madam! The items on my desk are not your concern. Kindly confine your interest to matters relevant to your future position.'

'I was only . . .'

'. . . inquisitive!' he snapped, thrusting the map into a drawer then slamming it shut so that the huge desk vibrated.

Georgina sighed.

His lips were firm. 'There's one lesson you've learned before we're even started. Now, about the journey . . .'

Despite his reluctance for having her accompany him to Scotland, Howard Saunders had given considerable attention to details for the visit and their plans were concluded with quiet efficiency. She began to relax, sensing that he would take good care of her.

As he walked with her through the hall, he seemed preoccupied. At the outer door he gazed down at her.

'I assume you have observed that it is January,' he remarked sharply. 'You needs must forget your appearance and concentrate on keeping out the cold. Scotland's a long way to the north, remember. You'd best equip yourself with a quantity of warm undergarments.'

Georgina nodded, but said nothing but a quiet 'good-bye' in response to his own.

It was snowing now, flakes fluttering down from a steely sky. Reflecting on Howard Saunders' admonition regarding her clothing, she was smiling to herself when Roland emerged from his carriage to assist her inside.

Georgina sensed his gaze quizzing her and took her time arranging first skirts and then her pelisse before she answered him.

'You appear inordinately pleased with yourself,' he commented. 'I see the fellow gave you an easy time of it.'

'On the contrary,' she retorted. 'He was prejudiced to the point of rudeness, and quite determined that no woman should assist him.'

'Ah.' His tone softened and he eased himself more comfortably on to the seat, then patted her arm. 'Do not fret, Georgina, I will give you what comfort . . .'

'That was initially,' she interrupted swiftly, for now she was close to erupting her news.

Roland stifled a groan. 'You're going with the fellow then?'

'Oh, yes — I am going.'

'Going off, unchaperoned. I'll thank you to recall that it is as an artist that you're to prove yourself!'

'Roland.'

'You need not sound shocked. I cannot imagine how you can even contemplate the excursion with a man you do not know. And you such a . . . such . . . well, you know how

21

long I've been urging you to bring forward our wedding date.'

Georgina sighed. 'I will settle in our home with you, and gladly, once I have done this.'

'How very gracious,' he snarled, sounding quite unlike even-tempered Roland. 'And what am I to do while you're away? Wait in Sevenoaks, I suppose, praying that the man has the decency to keep his hands from you!'

'Roland!'

'No, Georgina, you will hear me out. I have to speak, don't you see? Before it is too late. If you do come back from this preposterous venture nothing'll be the same. I doubt your dear mama will have acquainted you with the dangers that you'll face, it is my duty to inform you of them.'

'There is no need.' Georgina drew up her collar and leaned into the corner of the juddering carriage.

'There is need, my dear.' His sombre tone and the troubled light in his eyes won her attention, and some sympathy.

'You're a lovely girl, Georgina. Any man with blood flowing through him is bound to . . . to desire you.'

'Howard Saunders thinks only of his work.'

'That's as may be when he's at his desk. But what of the long hours you'll be sitting as we are sitting now, close beside each other?'

'He spoke of travelling by mail coach, we shall not be alone.'

'Oh. Oh well . . . But then there will be the nights, putting up at coaching inns.'

'You're not accusing me of wishing to share his room, I hope?'

'No, dearest, no. But . . .'

'But you should remember that it takes two persons to connive at such an arrangement, and I have no intention of relinquishing to another something that I am preserving for *our* wedding night.'

Roland nodded, suddenly unable to speak further. For all her determination to follow her chosen course, Georgina was such an innocent, so oblivious of the desires that could drive a man close to desperation. As he was being driven, at this moment, by having her this near and knowing the approaching end of his daily contact with her.

'You should not worry so, my dear,' she said. 'Howard Saunders will be as preoccupied elsewhere as I am myself. He introduced me to a fetching beauty, so exciting that I feel sure he doesn't really see any other woman.'

Roland appeared reassured, but he remained subdued until their arrival at

Georgina's home adjoining the boundary of Knole Park.

Her sisters, Amy and Emily, greeted them at the door, begging at once for news of her visit to London, and leading them into the drawing room. Before answering them, she went to kiss their mother whose solemn brown eyes ranged over her eldest daughter's face.

'Georgina,' she gasped, reading the exhilaration there, 'oh, Georgina, you are embarking on this — this journey, are you not?'

'Yes, Mama. I am sorry that it displeases you, but I feel that the time has come to think of pursuing my occupation . . .'

'Occupation! Don't you know of the long nights I've lain sleepless, praying that you would see sense? If only you'd wait until your father was home, he'd talk this notion out of your silly head. He will be here in a few days now, Georgina, I've had word today. You'd not wish to miss him, would you?'

Georgina swallowed. 'No, Mama, I trust that he will be safely home before I leave.'

Despairingly, Mrs Morton glanced up to her future son-in-law.

Roland shook his head. 'I have tried, Mrs Morton, but your daughter will heed no one.'

Wearily, Georgina's mother sighed and put a hand to her head. The two younger girls were chattering excitedly, their dark heads gleaming in the firelight as they darted and bobbed, eager to learn all they could. As soon as she decently dared, Georgina fled to her room.

The following three days continued in similar pattern, with Roland excusing himself from his uncle's legal practice to become a regular visitor.

Perturbed, Georgina occupied herself in sorting her artist's materials and packing clothes in readiness for visiting Scotland. She blessed the fact that her father's return from the Peninsular campaign would cheer her dear mama and give her young sisters an excitement to distract them from her own plans.

She rose before dawn on the morning that her father was expected, going to the kitchen where Nannie Meg, who had helped raise the three girls and had stayed on in the household, was supervising Nellie, one of the maids, as she lit the kitchen range.

'You're awake early, Miss Georgina,' Nannie Meg remarked. 'Is it conscience maybe that's keeping back the sleep?'

Georgina smiled and gave her the glance that had never quite succeeded in winning

her beloved Nannie into blind acquiescence.

'You know me too well!'

'Perhaps I do — and perhaps if your
mama knew you better she'd understand
that she'll not curb your determination. *And*
that she's no cause to fear that you'll do
aught that you shouldn't.'

Georgina's smile widened. 'I hoped you'd
know how I feel.'

Nannie Meg's laugh was close to a cackle.
'You need *one,* do you, Miss Georgina —
one who's on your side?'

Before she could respond, a sudden jan-
gling at the bell beside the front door accompanied by thumping upon its oaken
panels startled them.

'That must be father, earlier than we expected, I will let him in.'

'That's right, my love,' Nannie Meg called
after her. 'My old legs are slow wakening of
a morning, you'll be there more quickly.'

The chill of early morning marble struck
through her thin soles as Georgina ran
through the hall, experiencing a curious
mixture of elation and anxiety. Her dear father would hear all too soon of her intended
departure, and his attitude towards her
could well lose some of its unreserved affection.

As she drew back the iron bolts she breathed deeply. She must give him the warmest welcome ever — and thus allow them both a short period at least of their customary harmony.

Opening the door, Georgina felt snow falling in to drench her slippered toes and glanced briefly downwards before looking at the man who stood out on the steps. When she raised her eyes to those that were regarding her keenly she gasped.

This was no loving parent returning from the war, but an unsmiling man whom she'd never expected to see in her home surroundings.

Howard Saunders doffed his top hat. 'Miss Morton, forgive me. I come in haste and ask that you, if you're determined still, will accompany me with equal haste.'

Georgina blinked uncomprehendingly. 'I . . . do not understand.'

He sighed, and gestured impatiently. He looked exhausted.

'Please,' she said, 'come inside . . .'

He followed her into the hall and waited while she closed the door.

'What is it?' she asked.

'I am sorry, but matters have arisen making it imperative that I leave.' He paused, corrected himself: 'That I travel to

27

Scotland immediately.'

'Now — today?'

'Yes. It is essential that I leave this morning.'

'This morning?' she echoed.

He nodded. Again, he sighed. He appeared to be greatly agitated.

'I started out during the night. If you still wish to join me I must request that we set out at once.'

Perturbed by his sudden appearance and his urgency, Georgina hesitated.

'Well?' Mr Saunders prompted her. His anxiety lent added sharpness to the blue eyes.

She smiled. 'I will be ready to go with you within an hour.'

CHAPTER TWO

Howard Saunders appeared surprisingly at ease warming himself before the Bodley Range which made the kitchen the only comfortable room at this hour of the morning.

Georgina had been alarmed by the chill of his hand as she'd taken hat and coat from him, but soon Nannie Meg was pressing him to sip her strong hot tea.

'You look fair frozen to the marrow,' Nannie had admonished him, her ancient hazel eyes brightening in response to his courteous greeting. And she'd called back Georgina from the door before she could disappear to pack her belongings.

'You'll eat a good breakfast, my girl, the way I've always taught you, or you'll not leave this house. And if you cannot pack your possessions fast enough to suit this young gentleman, Old Nannie's the one who'll be helping you.'

'But there's so much to do, Nannie Meg,' Georgina protested, 'and I haven't even told Mama yet.'

'And I'll warrant your mama will be all

the better for being unable to dwell on your departure. Your father will be home directly you are gone, and he'll give her no time for sitting brooding.'

'Your father's coming home today, is he?' Mr Saunders enquired, his expression controlled.

Georgina nodded. 'I told you he was with Sir Arthur Wellesley, he's recently returned from fighting in Portugal.'

Howard Saunders said nothing. He seemed preoccupied.

'You — you're not feeling unwell are you?' Georgina asked.

'No — why should I be? I am concerned to be away, that is all. We have a long journey ahead of us, in unfavourable conditions.'

As soon as they had eaten, Georgina left Mr Saunders in Nannie Meg's care and went up to her room. Going rapidly through cupboards and drawers, she flung items of clothing together, hoping that a smoothing iron would be provided at their destination. She turned next to pens, pencils and brushes, checking that she had all that she might require before securing them in their box. Lastly she attended to the things necessary for her toilette and each overnight stay which, together with a change of undergarments, must be kept to hand during the journey.

She paused to stare hard at the bright-eyed features and flushed cheeks confronting her in the glass. Now she must steel herself to bid goodbye to her mother.

Georgina knocked, hesitantly, upon the door of her mother's room. 'Come in, my dear. See — I have a new coverlet for your father's homecoming, fresh curtains also . . .'

'Mama, please — please listen to me. I have to go, now, at once.'

'Go? Go, where?'

'To Scotland, Mother. Mr Saunders is here — has come for me. His plans are changed and . . .'

'Oh, Georgina, no!'

Her mother wept and cajoled and railed at her, until Georgina was compelled to close her ears. She'd endure no more of hearing that she was a disgrace to the family; an ungrateful daughter with no thought for her parents. And, returning to the hall, Georgina discovered Howard Saunders in no better humour, glaring towards the clock. Glancing around for her brown velvet pelisse, she found he was holding it for her. She slipped her arms into the closely-fitted sleeves.

'Thank you,' she said, warmed by the gesture, but when she turned to smile at him his blue eyes seemed dead as stone.

Emily and Amy ran to fling themselves at their sister in a frenzy of hugging and kissing, so that she felt suddenly that leaving her family would prove unbearable.

Nannie Meg was risking a chill by stepping out into the snow of the front steps and Georgina noticed Mr Saunders taking the old lady's hand while he spoke gravely. And then he was at her side, holding the carriage door for her, and sighing impatiently while Amy and Emily indulged in another round of kissing.

'You do intend leaving here, I assume?' he snapped.

Swallowing down an enormous lump in her throat, she allowed him to assist her into the fine carriage. Then they were hurtling along the drive, while she tried in vain to obtain a final glimpse of her sisters and Nannie Meg.

Leaning back into the upholstered seat, Georgina closed her eyes, distressed by upsetting her mother, and leaving Sevenoaks before her father's homecoming. Quelling a sigh, she breathed deeply. She must not weep.

Opening her eyes, she gazed about the

beautifully upholstered interior of his carriage.

'I am sure this couldn't have been furnished more pleasingly, you are to be complimented.'

'Not I,' he responded coolly, 'the carriage, a Berlin, is loaned from my cousin.'

'Oh. I thought — well, it seems as splendid as the home where you interviewed me.'

He was staring through the window to the snow-covered fields and did not trouble to glance her way.

'The house is not mine either. It belongs to Lady Virginia.'

'I see.'

'Whether or not you do is inconsequential.'

Georgina felt deflated by his indifference, yet she sensed that her companion was no happier than she herself. Inexplicably, she longed to cheer him.

'You have told me only that your book features Scotland. Won't you tell me more? I'm eager to learn which particular area it covers.'

'The area is wide, Miss Morton, embracing both Highland and Lowland country. But you need concern yourself only with the Lowlands. James MacInnes completed the etchings of the Highlands.'

'But you've written the entire book already, that is what you told me? I imagine you were longing to get the words down, weren't you?'

He gave her a curious glance but made no answer.

'Oh, isn't it all so exciting,' she cried. 'I have so *ached* to be able to show everyone how lovely the countryside is. If I can only reproduce one perfect scene so that I capture the splendour of the original, I shall be so happy.'

'I was of the impression,' he remarked dryly, 'that you were accompanying me in order to illustrate the remainder of my book, not to produce one picture to perfection.'

'If you knew how long I have waited for just this opportunity.'

'Has no one ever remarked upon your unfailing enthusiasm, Miss Morton?'

She laughed. 'Perhaps — but, of late, I fear that was meant reprovingly.'

He smiled, yet something about his features remained wintry as the rolling hills beyond their carriage.

'You're unhappy,' Georgina commented. 'I don't believe you want me with you at all.'

'Have I said that?'

'Your demeanour has. I only hope I can

prove, with time, that your initial impression was ill-founded.'

'You did yourself a disservice by deceiving me regarding your sex.'

Georgina sighed and for a while was silent. Glancing occasionally towards her companion, she observed that he seemed remote and preoccupied. His lips were drawn down at the corners and a frown furrowed the handsome forehead. Concerned, she wondered if something other than her presence was troubling him.

Mr Saunders remained distant when they stopped to take coffee in Greenwich and as Henry, the coachman, took up the reins again her employer spoke only to say that they were heading for the north of London.

'There we shall take the mail coach onward towards York.'

'I thought perhaps we would be staying the night in London.'

'No, I must ensure that we make the best possible speed northwards.'

'We shall be staying at a coaching inn then?'

'You sound apprehensive. Don't tell me the earnest traveller is experiencing misgivings!'

'No, of course not. I simply wished to know what I might expect.'

His wry laugh crackled about the carriage. 'You will soon learn, my dear young lady, that the *un*expected is what is most likely to occur.'

'Good. I have always hoped my dull existence would be enlivened by adventure.'

'I will remind you of that when you turn to me in fright.'

Before Georgina could reply they were both startled by a horse and rider who galloped past the window then halted abruptly immediately ahead.

'What the . . . !' Howard exclaimed. Hands clenched, he inhaled sharply. 'Keep quite still,' he ordered, 'and say nothing.'

'But . . .' she began, her brief terror evaporating as she looked again to the rider now barring their way.

'I will deal with this,' Mr Saunders snapped. 'Henry,' he shouted to the coachman, 'drive on, man!'

Fear accelerated Howard's pulse as he sensed that the encounter he'd striven to avoid was inescapable now.

'No — wait,' Georgina protested.

'Be still, woman. Drive on, I say!'

'Please,' Georgina cried; grasping his arm, she felt him flinch. 'You don't understand. I know the man.'

He gasped.

'That is my fiancé, Roland Crowbrook.'

'Your . . . your . . . oh, God!' Mr Saunders put a hand to his forehead, his face white.

'Would you please find out what the fellow requires?' he demanded.

Georgina went to the door of the carriage where Roland, breathless from his ride, awaited her.

'What is it?' she asked, impatiently.

He glanced at Howard Saunders.

'Georgina, I must speak privately with you.'

'You cannot expect me to stand in the snow in kid shoes, Roland . . .'

'I do not. You're to return with me, let me help you on to Caspar's back . . .'

'Indeed not. I have told you my intention. I know my departure was earlier than anticipated, but that gives you no cause to come chasing after me as though I were an errant child.'

'Will you let me speak?' He drew her away from the carriage and out of Howard's hearing. 'Your father is home. He it is who has sent me to fetch you back. He knows of Saunders and says he is a most unsuitable escort.'

'I do not believe you, Roland. This is some ruse of yours. I won't have it. Father would have come after me himself if he'd had any knowledge concerning — concerning Mr Saunders.'

'Your father's exhausted with travelling, Georgina, that's the reason I volunteered.'

'What is this supposed tale that you carry?'

'That Saunders was made to flee from Portugal.'

'That he *what* . . . ?' she demanded, puzzled.

'Your father said he intended some evil there. You must not continue . . .'

'This is nonsense. A fiction contrived to have me change my mind.'

Roland took a note from his pocket. He sighed as he handed it to her.

'I had hoped your trust in me would have proven sufficient without this. You'll see it is in your father's hand.'

Bewildered, Georgina read:

My dear daughter,
I was horrified to learn of your departure with Mr Howard Saunders, and thank God that I returned in time to despatch Roland in all haste to your rescue. Believe me, my dear, Saunders has placed himself in such disrepute in the Peninsular that all who served under Wellesley's command could only sympathize with the Portuguese for accelerating

his expulsion. Trust Roland who is worthy as ever and do not hesitate, but ride swiftly home to those who love you.

'Come, dearest, let us recover your possessions from his carriage and be rid of him . . .'

Georgina shook her head. 'I simply do not believe it. Roland, what is this? Some scheme to discredit Mr Saunders. Father does not even say what he has done.'

'Miss Morton,' Howard Saunders shouted from the door of the carriage as he waited on its step, 'are we to linger all day long while you bid adieu to every one of your relatives and acquaintances?'

'One moment please,' she responded, glancing from her employer's challenging gaze to her fiancé's anxious face.

'Tell me, Roland, what is it that he has done?'

'I know only what is in your father's letter.'

'Miss Morton, has this glimpse of your betrothed proved more appealing than the work which you claimed was of such importance?'

The challenge from the carriage made her swing round indignantly. She was on the point of showing Mr Saunders her father's note and demanding an explanation. Intuition, however, had her crumple the paper instead; and the magnetism that she'd recognized in his eyes seemed to draw her to him. Somehow, without her willing assent, her legs were taking her towards him. Her pace quickening with every step, sure-footed over the icy ground, she walked away from Roland.

She felt pulses speeding her feet and now only the slippery ground prevented her from running. And all the while she sought the approval in the blue eyes rivetting her attention. Nearing him, she gasped, his fine features and golden hair appeared so splendid.

His hand was warm through her gloves, his arm firm at her waist, as he assisted her into the carriage. It was only then that Georgina became aware of Roland calling her name.

Howard raised a querying eyebrow and his gaze clouded. She glanced over her shoulder to find Roland behind her.

'Thank Father for his concern,' she said quietly. 'I will write to reassure him. You may tell him that he has no cause for worry.'

'But, Georgina . . .' Roland persisted.

Turning to her companion, she nodded.

'Drive on, Henry,' Mr Saunders ordered, and Roland was left sitting astride his stallion, motionless.

Georgina slipped the crumpled note inside her glove and tried to calm the thudding of her heart. Howard Saunders was smiling.

'You've a mind of your own then, young Georgina, and an admirable spirit!'

She smiled back and knew that her eyes shone. Howard's hand was at her sleeve, caressing the velvet and stirring tremors within her.

'I wonder that the fellow let you go,' he said, his tone soft. 'Those magnificent eyes are so enhanced when you're perturbed, no real man could turn away.'

Abruptly, he drew away into his own corner of the carriage. He had travelled scarcely thirty miles with the girl and already feelings that he'd meant to discipline surged through him. Had the shock of being accosted and fear of having her leave him shattered reasoning? Where were the wits that had brought him safely home from Portugal? He'd require a cool head still to keep ahead of those who sought him.

Despite his resolve, his glance went to the girl. Georgina. A regal name for one who had the bearing of a princess. Her home, though larger than he'd expected, had seemed unpretentious, yet it had bred this creature who possessed more dignity than many women of his acquaintance. May the respect she'd aroused in him ensure he protect her — and not least from his own desires.

Georgina was subdued by her employer's sudden withdrawal. His thin face had grown sombre, excluding her.

Fearful that Howard Saunders possessed some uncanny power that was released by just one glance towards his attractive features, she wondered if she'd been mesmerized into continuing this journey. Her father must have had good reason for sending Roland after her, had she been incautious?

They dined that night in Huntingdon. Georgina was exhausted. Indeed, she'd been hardly conscious of her surroundings since they had joined the mail coach to the north of London. There, Mr Saunders had despatched his cousin's Berlin — and with it, apparently, all pretence of conversation. They had sat with four other passengers in silence. Perplexed by her companion, anxiety, also, had added its toll.

'Only a little further and then we'll put up for the night.'

Howard Saunders had risen from the table, and was heading towards the door of the inn.

'But . . .'

'Yes?' His tone was impatient, his eyes sharp as he turned.

Georgina stifled her protest. He had warned her the journey would be hard, he'd not receive the satisfaction of learning that she wilted already. Drawing her coat about her against the icy blast from the open door, she smiled.

'I haven't complimented you on selecting so — so adequate a hostelry for our evening meal,' she exclaimed quickly.

As he held the door for her, she felt his curious gaze but kept her eyes lowered. His glance could conceal his thoughts while her own proved all too transparent.

The bugle sounded before the mail coach reached the inn, and with its note Georgina felt excitement dispelling all tiredness. Its wheels seemed to thunder as the coach slowed on the courtyard cobbles.

The coach gleamed, its paint and harness brilliant in the light from the inn. Georgina felt entirely recovered from any misgivings regarding her future — all she wanted was to be carried away by this splendid conveyance. Her new life was beginning.

Howard Saunders' preoccupation was with the other passengers. As when they'd joined the other coach, he scrutinized everyone carefully. And then he withdrew into his corner, turning his face towards the darkness outside.

When they stopped at Peterborough, her relief that it was time to rest superseded all other emotions. Weary, and grimacing with soreness from sitting too long, Georgina scarcely noticed the manner in which Howard's glance raked round the inn before he addressed the landlord. It would be several days before her memory yielded up his strange behaviour.

Sleepily, she bade him goodnight and only her upbringing compelled her to check the cleanliness of the sheets before she slipped between them.

Her awakening was earlier and more sudden than she would have chosen. Darkness still hugged the inn when a hot jug was brought to her room.

The serving maid smiled sympathetically at Georgina's disordered appearance.

'I'm right sorry, miss, to wake you, but Mr Saunders is at breakfast already and bids you be a-stirring.'

Georgina yawned, thanking the girl, then staggered about the room on aching limbs. How she would endure a further day's travelling and then another, she could not imagine.

Howard remained aloof throughout the

day. All evidence of the momentary warmth towards her had vanished. She wondered if she could have dreamed his compliments upon the quality of her eyes. For surely this man was scarcely aware that she was a woman.

Once only did he relax sufficiently to make her smile, as they were re-joining the mail coach after a pause for fresh horses. Her expression had evidently revealed her discomfort after sitting for the best part of two days, and he smiled wryly as a hand went to her elbow.

'If you had heeded my advice regarding thick undergarments you would have benefited from having your personal upholstery.'

Her blush rose right the way from her bosom to discount the effect of the keen wind hurling snowflakes about them. But his eyes, when she risked a glance, rewarded her with the humour that she loved to see there.

'Tomorrow you shall enjoy a brief respite,' he promised. 'I have business during the morning in York.'

York would have delighted Georgina had she been granted an opportunity for exploring the city. As it was, she had to content herself with glimpses of its walls and great Minster after luncheon as they set out in a borrowed travelling carriage.

She hoped that this was not setting the pattern for their travels. Surely Howard Saunders realized that she could not be expected to wait around in her room at some coaching inn, emerging only when he could escort her, and that mere glimpses would not suffice for her to make her sketches?

She had found the morning boring and, worse, had wondered yet again how right her father had been in believing Mr Saunders untrustworthy. He had appeared restless and apprehensive throughout their journey this far.

The weather over the Yorkshire moors was as formidable as the lowering landscape. The wind that had seemed sharp in the city wailed past the carriage, buffeting them and whirling snow into drifts to either side of the narrow track. Howard's meeting that morning must have been reassuring. He enquired now, with an all too rare twinkle in his blue eyes, if she were feeling more comfortable after her rest at the inn.

Georgina laughed with him, explaining that much of her time there had been spent in sitting also.

'You'll very likely be longing for the chance to do just that before the week is out. I'll work you hard, north of the border. And many's the occasion there'll be nowhere even to lean your back while you're busy with pencil and paper.'

She responded, 'I wish only to begin the task.'

He nodded and then sighed, 'I envy you your clear eyes and open heart, young lady, and the spirit that has no cause to fear any man.'

Georgina smiled uneasily, sensing some darkness that clung about him. And, in that moment when he turned teasingly towards her, she acknowledged her unreserved liking for this man. If only she were able to trust him implicitly.

The lurching as the horse stumbled on a patch of ice had her grasping instinctively for her companion's hand. Comforted by the strength of his grasp, she felt reassured, until she saw his frown.

'Confound it!' he muttered.

Georgina saw that the horse's hoof, caught in the deeply rutted surface, had twisted. In obvious pain, the animal stumbled to a halt, dragging the carriage into the thick snow of the wayside ditch.

The coachman came over anxiously to consult Mr Saunders. 'I'm that sorry, sir, but we can't go on. Yon's a faithful mare, but she's hurt real bad, I reckon. I daresn't urge her on till she's had attention.'

'You're right of course,' agreed Howard Saunders.

'Happen they'll have a horse to spare over the hill yonder, in Longwold. I'll walk on there, if you'd bide here with the young lady.'

'Surely.'

'I'll be quick as I'm able. I know one of the grooms at Dale Farm, he'll be glad to help us.'

'Thank heavens this didn't happen further south,' Howard Sanders exclaimed as they watched the coachman plodding off.

Puzzled, Georgina glanced sideways at her companion. 'It would have been warmer there, and less snow to isolate us.'

'That is what I meant. I don't know what I was thinking . . .'

But he *had* known, Georgina felt sure; he had been relieved to be this distant from London before anything delayed their flight. *Flight,* that was it, she thought. It had been so eloquent in his behaviour since, arriving at her home. She was compelled to admit Howard's conduct was that of a hunted man.

Why, only a moment before he'd spoken of his inability to feel free of fear.

'Poor Georgina. You must be very cold.'

He was smiling down at her, the blue eyes that always seemed so compelling were concerned now. She swallowed, trying to quieten the trembling that owed nothing to the weather.

'I'm not quite certain where we are,' he continued. 'I only hope our coachman finds his way to Longwold.' He stopped speaking suddenly and pointed into the broad valley where the river, silvered with frost, meandered, scarcely discernible against the white blanket.

'Do you see — there, beside the river. There's an abbey. This side nearest to us is ruined, but some of the outer buildings seem intact. It could be inhabited still, if only by someone acting as warden.'

He faced her.

'You don't appear at all upset Miss Morton.'

'We are in the dry and quite comfortable.'

'And you don't even complain of the cold. But would you be afraid if I left you alone — just for a short while — long enough for me to run as far as the abbey and ask their assistance?'

She smiled, delighted by his genuine interest in her welfare.

'I shall sit here quietly, awaiting your return. The abbey is near enough, and I shall watch until you are admitted.'

Turning up the collar of his coat, he gave

her another searching glance, then set out from the carriage. In minutes, Georgina saw him disappear among the abbey ruins.

Howard had just gone from sight when she heard hooves clattering behind the carriage along the frozen track. She smiled ruefully, thinking that their coachman had secured a horse and Howard might have spared himself.

The glass of the window splintered with a snap, and a pistol jerked to within inches of her throat.

Before she could utter a cry, a swarthy face, the eyes scarlet-rimmed from cold, thrust through the opening.

'Hand over your jewels, money as well . . . !'

Georgina's fingers flew to her throat. The fellow pushed them aside with the pistol as his other hand went to the catch and opened the door. Swiftly, he dismounted and climbed, smirking, into the carriage. He was a huge man, tall and muscular. The watery eyes ran over her person, assessing her wealth, while he adjusted the gun's aim to her breast.

He seized her hands, tearing the gloves from them. When he saw her ring he chuckled.

'No, no!' she cried, and struggled. Iron hard fingers clamped on to her ring, as he wrestled to drag it from her hand. Writhing, Georgina fought him but, leaving her knuckles bleeding, he slid the ring into his pocket.

Next his gaze found the amethyst brooch at her décolletage. Snatching it from her gown, he ripped the delicate ecru material.

'So, here's your real treasure, eh? Not in gold or jewels, of which you've precious few, but in a body ripe for the plucking!'

Georgina screamed.

'Ah, yes — you'll serve me well. And there, indeed, is a sort of justice. For yours is the coachman, I'll be bound, who interrupted my pleasure in the stables back yonder.'

She tried pushing him from her; she might equally have attempted to shift the fell that overshadowed them.

'I cursed him for bursting in, but he's brought me fresher game than that flighty wench who's any man's.'

'Please, please — no!' Georgina gasped as he pocketed his pistol, leaving both hands free.

She shuddered as icy fingers thrust inside her torn gown to cup her breast. And then he lunged towards her and she felt the scrub of whiskery chin against her face. His other hand was on her thigh, working over the thin satin.

CHAPTER THREE

The man's breath was heavy with the odour of liquor, and coming in urgent gasps. Georgina was terrified, fighting to keep his great body from her own. Her struggles had left her leaning awkwardly into one corner, now she seemed about to suffocate as he pressed his bulk against her.

The seat was too narrow, the carriage too confining for his purpose. He cursed, glancing feverishly about while his hands continued their fumbling.

Suddenly, he snorted, full lips curling in satisfaction. As he eased himself away from her, Georgina sprang from her corner, but he seized her wrist and dragged her to him.

'You're coming with me,' he announced, as he hauled her from the carriage and on to the horse. Mounting behind her, he tugged on the reins and turned off the road.

Furrowing through snow drifts, he forced his mount on towards the abbey ruins. Georgina closed her eyes, praying they might meet Howard.

They met no one. It seemed only seconds

before the brute was pulling her from his horse. They were enclosed now by high walls, open to the sky. The man yanked her towards him again and slithered a hand inside her coat, to linger once more over the soft texture of her breast. He moaned, as though from some ache, and she sensed him glancing behind her.

And then he was edging her backwards, fingers biting through her sleeve to prevent her escaping.

The glacial stone of a tomb chilled the back of her legs as his thighs seared into the base of her stomach. The man's mouth found hers and when she sank her teeth into his lip he only laughed, transferring wet kisses to her neck.

His fingers were fumbling at her skirts, the eyes so close to her face appeared glazed, his breathing rapid. Instinct warned her his next move would be to loosen his own clothing.

She screamed, almost fracturing her spine against the tombstone as she struggled.

His hand stung her across the mouth. 'Try that once more and I'll shoot you first then have my way while you're still warm.'

Georgina kicked out at his shins then bent her knee, thrusting it into his groin. He staggered backwards, groaning, and she fell trembling against the tomb. Recovering quickly, he lunged upon her again.

Howard's hand appeared above them, he seized the man's collar, and punched him fiercely on the chin. And then he turned to Georgina as she cowered beside the tomb.

Going down on one knee, he placed a hand on her shoulder.

'Georgina — has the villain harmed you?'

Mutely, she shook her head. The man hauled himself to his feet and tottered towards his mount.

'Shouldn't we . . . try to stop him?' Georgina murmured.

'It'd take more than the two of us to hold him. He's a rogue well-known in these parts.'

His glance went to her legs as she tried to cover them with her skirt.

'Then why is he permitted to . . . ?'

'. . . roam the moors, robbing . . . ? He's a crafty customer who finds a route out of any gaol. But I'll make sure he's arrested now.'

Georgina gulped, clutching her pelisse about her to hide the tears in her gown.

Howard helped her to her feet, supporting her with an arm.

'Let's return to the carriage. You are certain that he didn't hurt you?'

'Not seriously. I am bruised and scratched but no worse than that.'

Howard carried her through the snow-covered meadow. He was setting her down beside their carriage when the coachman appeared astride a borrowed horse.

'I'm to leave our own mare at the farm as we go by, sir,' he told Howard before noticing the broken window in the carriage door. 'Has there been trouble?'

'I am afraid so. I went seeking help and in my absence Dawson o' the Moors came this way . . .'

'You don't mean . . .' He glanced towards Georgina and led Howard aside. 'Did he harm the young lady?'

Howard shook his head. 'Fortunately, she managed to fight him off.'

Shaking, Georgina huddled on the seat, scarcely noticing as the two men replaced the injured horse and hauled the carriage back on to the track.

Howard rode outside with the coachman as far as the next hamlet. He informed the authorities about Dawson o' the Moors, arranged a temporary repair of the window and then joined Georgina.

She was trembling still.

'You understand now why I advised against you coming.'

'I knew you'd say that! Next you'll be telling me you are sending me home.'

'Taking you, my dear, *taking* — back to Kent when we've both had a night's sleep.'

'To prove yourself right and me wrong, so that you can go on thinking I am no good at anything. Just because I am not a man.' She pulled away from him and her velvet pelisse slid open. She glanced down. One breast, bare and covered in scratches, was thrusting from her high-waisted gown which had been ripped almost to her sash. Shocked and embarrassed, tears filled her eyes as she hastily drew the brown velvet across her.

'You are hurt,' he protested, for he had seen the deep scratches on her peach-soft skin.

'It is nothing,' she murmured.

'An unclean wound that may fester.'

'I'll see it is cleansed when we reach our night's lodging.'

'That may be too late.'

'Please — let me alone.'

'I'll not harm you. On long journeys I carry a flask of water, let me bathe . . .'

'No. No!' His tenderness released the pent-up shock and all at once she was sobbing, clutching her pelisse, chilled, but not by the air penetrating the hurriedly-repaired window.

Firm fingers untwined her own from the velvet.

Howard drew in a sharp breath. He moistened a freshly-laundered handkerchief and began easing away the streaks of blood.

Georgina closed her eyes. With the silk soothing her sore skin her sobbing quietened, but touched by his concern, she couldn't check her tears. When she opened her eyes her hand went instinctively to smooth the fair hair as he bent over her.

Howard glanced up. 'Almost finished now . . .'

He drew the ecru material over her breasts, fastening it with the pin from his neckcloth. He wrapped the coat about her, turning up its collar, his hands lingering while he gazed into her eyes, his expression unfathomable.

'Thank you,' she whispered, and smiled. Yesterday, he'd been a stranger; interesting, exciting, but someone of whom she was cautious. Today, he'd proved himself a friend. Her thanks seemed so . . . inadequate. Impulsively, she turned and touched his cheek with her lips.

For one second Howard remained motionless, still scrutinizing her, then strong hands slid around her shoulders. His kiss was tentative at first, but soon his lips were disturbing, urging her response. His nearness made her dizzy, and her own body stirred with an eagerness as strong as the revulsion she'd felt before for the man who had attacked her. And she knew this eagerness was more dangerous.

Howard raised his head. The blue eyes held her gaze for one minute, two . . . and then he drew away.

'I don't usually embrace a young lady on such short acquaintance,' he said. 'You must forget the incident.'

'So, now you're more convinced than ever that I must be returned immediately to my mother!'

'*Now?*' he demanded. 'If you think I have no control over my emotions you're much mistaken.'

Georgina erased her smile. 'I'm certain you have excellent self-restraint. Unless you fear I have less . . .'

'You know the reasons — have learned one hazard of travelling.'

'Force me to return to Kent and I'll never be certain that you weren't afraid of our continuing proximity.'

'You've a high estimation of your own appeal!'

Georgina inhaled sharply. The remark was unfair, hadn't he kissed her only moments ago?

'I don't care whether you approve my

person,' she snapped. 'But I do care about my profession. I don't like leaving anything unfinished.'

She thought he muttered: 'I can believe that,' but she let the comment pass.

'There are matters to settle before your departure,' he said coldly. 'Did that fellow Dawson rob you as well?'

Aghast, Georgina retailed the amethyst brooch and her ring. How ever would she explain their loss to her fiancé.

'He took my ring and a brooch.'

'Valuable?'

'To me.'

'I'll attend to their replacement.'

'You shall not.'

'I left you unprotected.'

'You made adequate amends. I said from the first that you were not responsible for me.'

'H'm.' He sounded sceptical, yet when night came and then the morning, no mention was made of her returning to Kent.

They reached Scotland with no further incident and made towards the home of friends of Howard Saunders just over the border. Wearied by travelling, Georgina could only make a pretence of enjoying the meal, out of consideration for their hosts. As Howard and Fraser Mallaig talked earnestly, she tried to keep awake.

Mr Mallaig was a gregarious man whose black hair and green eyes combined with sharp features to make his appearance compelling. His wife Isobel wore her dun-coloured hair dressed severely and, bulky with their first child, seemed to be always in her husband's shade.

Georgina wished her concentration was sharper when Howard began speaking of his work with an enthusiasm she'd not heard before.

One of his rare smiles enhanced the blue eyes. 'Maybe I should not be the one to say, Fraser, but this is my best yet. Had James MacInnes lived, we'd have created the finest book to guide people around Scotland.'

Frowning, Mr Mallaig glanced in Georgina's direction.

Howard inclined his head towards her. 'Miss Morton knows she's yet to prove herself. But I'm indebted to you, Fraser, for taking me through so much of your native countryside.'

'You had help from others, too.'

'Indeed. And have again. The Laird of Tocherd said I must stay with him whenever I returned. He's been in London on business, but I've written to his housekeeper and that's where we'll be staying.'

'Oh, that's a pity,' Isobel Mallaig said, looking across the table to Georgina. 'I was hoping you'd bide with us.'

'I'm grateful,' Howard responded quickly, 'but we need to be further to the west.'

Isobel smiled and nodded. 'Perhaps you'll be wanting to rest your horse and spend the night on your long journey home?'

'That's most kind. I'll look forward to returning.'

'We will indeed,' Georgina gave the quiet woman a warm smile.

'Have you see the Laird recently?' Howard enquired.

'Not since you were last with us. We'd a good night, hadn't we, the four of us?'

The men laughed together. And Howard Saunders appeared a different man to Georgina.

Abruptly, he sighed. 'But all the companionship's lost now. With James dead, this'll be a weary visit to Tocherd.'

'You say the Laird's away?'

'Mrs Whiting expects him back today.'

'Well, then . . .'

'I do not like change that affects my work.'

Fraser Mallaig sought Georgina's gaze.

'So you're the one now, Miss Morton, who'll be illustrating Howard's text. Have you had much experience?'

61

'I have been well taught by Professor Anstey, an illustrator. He coached me, and taught me engraving.'

'Which'll be wasted with me,' Howard snapped.

Fraser glanced sideways at him, then back to Georgina.

'And I believe Howard approved samples of your work?'

'Yes, I was very . . .' She was about to say 'fortunate' when her employer interrupted.

'She tricked her way in — signing herself *Geo.* Morton, or I'd never have considered her.'

Georgina bit her lip. So that still rankled.

Fraser smiled again. 'Well, I'm delighted Howard has brought us such an attractive guest.'

'The choice was forced upon me,' Howard said sharply. 'No one else applied.'

Deflated, Georgina would have excused herself, but Fraser Mallaig compensated for his friend's ill-humour by flirting with her until she feared Isobel might be offended.

As they travelled on towards Tocherd, Howard remained taciturn. Georgina wondered how on earth she would endure the days spent co-operating with him over the book. But endure she would; she'd prove herself the equal of Mr MacInnes.

Tocherd Castle dominated the glen that bore its name, and seemed to Georgina the most enchanting place that she'd ever seen. The snow had ceased, clearing the skies so the sun glinted off frosted drifts to either side. Icicles fell from bare branches, tinkling like glassy fragments on to the hard ground.

'How splendid,' she exclaimed, expecting Howard to enthuse with her but, glancing sideways, she saw his frown. Was he wishing for different company? How he must regret the folly that had prompted him to kiss her.

Well, regrets were not *his* sole prerogative. Despite her tiredness, she had spent the night thinking about her own uncomfortable emotions. And had reached no conclusion. How could she, when she had enjoyed the wretched man's kisses, and at the same time was promised to Roland? Beneath her glove, her finger was sore still, reminding her of the stolen ring. How could she placate her fiancé, without admitting that he had foreseen the dangers she would face?

Tocherd Castle was larger than she'd anticipated, its sloping roofs soaring up from walls that looked stout as solid granite. Georgina had noticed how small its windows were but was unprepared for the darkness when the Laird's housekeeper led them into the great entrance hall. But Mrs Whiting's welcome augured a pleasant stay. The slight, middle-aged woman extended both hands to Howard.

'How good it is to see you, Mr Saunders. You're well, I hope?'

'Thank you, yes. Is the Laird not home?'

'Oh, bless you, he's back from London. He's out with the head man. But he'll be in soon and pleased to see you, I'll warrant. He'll have a surprise and all. I was after telling him you were on your way but he gave me no chance. You know you're always welcome here.'

Mrs Whiting had glanced towards Georgina; feigning annoyance, she eyed Howard severely.

'Will you not introduce me to your lady friend?'

As Howard did so, Georgina smiled. 'It was kind of you to welcome us here.'

'It's a poor sort of welcome so far, and you so cold. You'll both take a wee drop of whisky?'

Howard nodded, smiling. When Georgina would have demurred, he raised an eyebrow. 'Are you too fragile, Miss Morton, to withstand a warming drink?'

'Indeed not — I'll be delighted.'

If fire could liquefy then that, she felt sure, was what she gulped from the crystal glass.

'Very — very pleasant,' she mumbled, surprised her vocal chords were intact.

Mr Saunders seemed amused.

'I'll be showing you to your rooms . . .' Mrs Whiting began.

'You can take Miss Morton to hers. I'll wait and see your master as soon as he comes in.'

Georgina followed Mrs Whiting up the huge stone staircase hung with tapestries showing battle scenes. She glanced over the wrought-iron balustrade, to the open fireplace where logs crackled and spat and scarcely improved the temperature.

The housekeeper said, 'We're accustomed to the chill, but I fear you'll be uncomfortable. I've done my best with your room, though, there's been a fire in the grate since morning, and a warming pan in the bed.'

'You're very kind, thank you.'

'So, it's . . . *working* with Mr Saunders, you are?'

'Yes, I am an artist.'

'Oh, aye. Like Mr MacInnes before you.'

'I hope so, but Mr Saunders implies that Mr MacInnes was an incomparable paragon.'

'Well, there's a thing! Not that it was my business, mind — but many's the time I heard Mr Saunders criticising Mr Mac-Innes for being lazy.'

'I see . . .'

Mrs Whiting smiled as she opened a door in a long corridor. 'Maybe you're finding him a dour man at times?'

Georgina smiled, but said nothing.

Her room was high in one of the towers, large and oak-panelled, with several windows giving views over the snowy landscape towards a loch.

The bed, which appeared enormous, was canopied in velvet matching the red curtains.

'You'll find you're quite cosy once you're a-bed,' the housekeeper said. 'We've just completed these curtains and bed-hangings; there's little else to while away the long winters here.'

'They look beautiful. Is the castle very old?'

'Parts of Tocherd are older than Glamis itself, but some rooms were added last century. And the stable block replaces one destroyed during the Rebellion. Well, Miss Morton, you'll hear the gong for dinner. Before then one of the men will bring your baggage. I'll send Fiona with your hot jug, and tell her she's to help with your unpacking.'

'Thank you again.'

'If there's aught else you require you must tell Fiona.'

'I cannot imagine any improvement that could be made.'

Mrs Whiting gave her a beaming nod as she went out.

Georgina crossed to a window. The sun had long since sunk behind the hills, the flurries of snowflakes ended the interval between showers. Heavy clouds scudded across the sky and, as night fell swiftly, obliterated the view.

Turning away, she took up one of the silver candle holders, but before she had found tinder and flint she heard shouting from the hall below.

'You'll leave my home now,' a sharp Scots voice declared.

She hurried towards the long staircase.

'You cannot mean this,' her employer said, but a roar sliced his sentence.

'I'll thank ye to forget I ever knew you! Do you think I'd have for a friend one who turns traitor! You'll leave Tocherd. And you'd best be grateful I've no' had you flung into gaol . . .'

At the word 'traitor' Georgina froze and clutched the iron balustrade. The word echoed the warning from her father.

'I'd not dare sleep while you were under my roof!' the tough Scots voice went on. 'Scum like yourself would no' hesitate to put knife or bullet through an honest man.'

Georgina waited to hear no more. Quietly, she ran to her room, collected together the few belongings she had brought upstairs and flung on her pelisse.

Running towards the staircase again, she stopped. She had no wish to meet the angered Laird, and she was determined to leave Tocherd without Howard's knowledge.

A search revealed a corridor leading to the rear. She fled along its slippery boards, and ran unsteadily down another staircase.

Once she had escaped Tocherd she would head back towards the border. No matter that she had no transport. Better she trudge through ice and snow than spend another hour with a ruthless traitor.

The stairway seemed endless and was dark, for its granite walls had no windows. Georgina was almost at its foot when she stumbled and hurtled down the stone steps. Bruised and shaken, she landed in a tiny lobby.

A dog barked from beyond the walls, another somewhere above her.

Someone wrenched open a door near the top of the stair.

'Who's there?' a man called, 'who's there, I say!'

Terrified, Georgina remained silent, quivering, where she had fallen.

'Who's there?' he repeated. 'Answer, or I'll shoot!'

She was numb with fright.

At the report of a gun, she screamed and sprang to her feet, feeling her way around in search of a door.

'Don't move,' came the shout from above her head, 'or I'll kill you!'

Heavy boots began clattering down the stone steps towards her.

CHAPTER FOUR

Determined that she would not be discovered, Georgina frantically explored the rough walls, tearing her fingers as she searched for a door. At last her hands found wood, and then the latch and bolts.

The man's footsteps were clearer on the stair, and with them the swift padding of a dog. She seemed not to breathe as her ears strained for a second crack from the gun. The huge bolts moved with a rattle that made her shudder.

Out in the icy January night, Georgina blinked, trying to see something of her surroundings. And through the thickness of castle walls she heard those footsteps thundering down the stair.

She stood now in a courtyard. Through an archway the dwindling light revealed open ground. Against this snowy background she'd be easily seen. Keeping close in to the wall, she turned to her right. The building had shielded the paving from snow, leaving nothing to reveal tell-tale footprints.

An angle of the wall gave concealment as

she drew her gown and pelisse tight back into the shadows. The click of a latch made her jump.

The dog barked, then settled to a low growl. Her heart pounding, she stood listening.

A man snorted, so near that he could only be an arm's length from her. Georgina stilled her trembling lips.

'Heel, Boxer,' the man shouted. 'Back indoors with you; yon intruder'll be caught inside the estate boundary.' The door slammed shut and Georgina leaned, shaking, against the cold wall. So far she had escaped, but there would be other guards. What was more, somewhere in the darkness out there was Howard Saunders. From what she'd learned, he was more to be dreaded than Tocherd's men.

She began running. Her eyes were accustoming themselves to the odd light coming off the snow so that the blackness became less impenetrable. Her head felt dizzy, and she cursed the ease with which she had taken whisky without first eating. Her thin soles saturated, and slipping on the frozen ground, she scuttered towards the shelter of a nearby copse. Only wind rushing through bare branches disturbed the night. She paused, gasping in the freezing air, steadying her thumping heart. And then she was speeding forward again, all her senses straining for any sign that she wasn't alone.

'Georgina!'

The cry was to her left and near. She forced her aching legs to run on through the trees. Twigs snatched at her hair and snagged the velvet of her coat. Again she heard Howard.

'Georgina, *this* way, I'm over here . . .'

She could not let him reach her. He'd guess that she'd heard the Laird's accusation, and feel compelled to silence her.

She tripped over a snow-covered root and went sprawling.

'Wait — I'll help you.'

In panic, she realized that he must be sufficiently close to have seen her fall. She clawed at the tree trunk, hauling herself to her feet, then staggering forward.

'Georgina, not that way!' Howard cried, running to her.

At her side, he whirled her round to face him. He had been certain that he'd have to leave her at Tocherd as he fled. And he'd recognized in that instant that she was the one woman whose loss would unman him completely.

'Have they turned you out as well?' he demanded, 'terrifying you so that you run heedless away from the wretched place?'

She did not respond, but stared at him as though hypnotized. Even in the gloom here she could see the grey tinge of his features, that he was on the point of collapse. Yet alongside this concern for him had come the realization that it was from this man that she had fled, from him that she must flee. It must be of no consequence that she saw him suddenly as someone grown dear. *Traitor*, he had been called. And had not her own father warned her against him?

'Georgina, come — you are safe now.' He held her to him and, momentarily, she felt the comfort in his strong arms. But when she made as if to draw away again there was no escaping his grasp.

'I was afraid I'd never find you again,' he said and began hurrying her along with him. 'I have to leave tonight. Unhappily, the Laird can no longer give us accommodation. But I suspect you know that already — what did he say to you?'

Dumbly, Georgina shook her head.

'Explanations later,' Howard told her, 'the carriage isn't far and our coachman is re-loading our belongings.'

As he assisted her into the carriage, Georgina was bemused. If Howard Saunders meant to dispose of her he used strange methods.

'Come, we must hurry,' he said, 'the Laird's men are after us.'

She sat there silently. Her gaze towards the moonlit scene was fixed on Tocherd castle, and she still heard the words of the Laird.

'Do you think I'd have for a friend one who turns traitor!'

So clearly was the phrase repeated in her head that she glanced to see if her companion also heard it. He was sitting rigidly in his corner. His expression did, indeed, reveal apprehension, but he gave no sign of hearing the sentence that so obsessed her.

Georgina was calm now, although her thoughts still raced. She was being rushed she knew not where by this man whom she dared not trust. Yet how could she escape? Before the carriage stopped she would have to devise some plan that would ensure her safety.

All too quickly, Howard called their coachman to halt at a solitary inn. He turned to her.

'Here, I hope, we may find rooms for the night.'

Georgina could only follow as he descended from the carriage and went to knock on the tiny door. 'Aye?' The man who opened to them was dark-skinned from exposure to the keening winds. Georgina could not visualize the sun reaching this bleak place.

'We seek rooms for the night,' Howard began.

'Rooms?' the man repeated, scowling as he glanced from one to the other. 'I have but one room vacant.'

'We'll take it,' Howard was saying as Georgina started to protest.

The man stared calculatingly towards her. 'Is she your wife?'

Howard hesitated just long enough to arouse the innkeeper's suspicions.

'You're not wed, are you? Then I'll not accommodate you. I'd no' face the elders of the kirk if I connived as such wrong-doing.'

'But the lady's exhausted.'

'You can sit in one of the public rooms till the mail coach calls, but I'll have you out then, there's little enough room for customers wanting a meal.'

Georgina was trying to warm her fingers at the meagre fire when Howard's touch on her shoulder made her flinch.

'Georgina! You know I'd not harm you.'

He dropped his hands to his side. He'd been a fool to suppose . . . She wanted nothing, not even comfort, from him.

His eloquent eyes searched her face. The

hands that went to her shoulders seemed to give courage but she must not let him lull her into an unreal security.

'Don't blame me that we have no bed,' he snarled. 'If you'd given no sign we'd have had a room.'

Imagining the horror of being confined all night long with him, dreading that he might kill her, she shuddered.

His hands left her shoulders and he strode towards the window before facing her again.

'You see now how impossible it is that we travel like this. No one'll ever give us a night's lodging. Now the Laird's refused us, I must send you home.'

Now that he was the one to suggest her departure the escape for which she'd longed appeared a grim prospect. Could she so easily leave? Tired and more than a little frightened still, she blinked back tears of bewilderment.

Howard came back to her side. It was through him that she'd been turned from the castle and he'd never before seen her weep. His arm went about her shoulders but again she flinched. He stood away.

'You were right to be frightened when Dawson 'o the Moors would have had his way with you. And that's another reason we cannot continue as we are. You'd not be safe.'

'Safe?' she echoed. 'It isn't the fear of that incident that scares me . . .'

'Then it should,' he interrupted, angrily. If she'd not been so frightened by Dawson that she shrank from every man, it must be *his* touch that revolted her.

'Do you fear I'd take you?' he asked, his gaze hard. 'Without your consent? Is that it?'

'I do not believe that you would,' she stated dully.

'Then what in the Lord's name ails you?'

'Do you need to ask?' she demanded. 'You've been turned from Tocherd by a man who was once your friend!'

'They told you to leave as well, *and* the reason . . .'

'No.'

He regarded her keenly, obviously puzzled.

Sighing, Georgina went on: 'I heard the Laird — shouting . . .'

'How much did you hear? How much, Georgina?'

She dared not tell him.

'How much did you hear?' His voice was a roar, the blue eyes harsh.

'Enough.'

'Enough to doubt me, like everyone else.'

Earlier, he had been shocked by his own dread of losing her. Now his anguish had a different source. She too, distrusted him.

'Explain his words then, tell me why he called you . . .' She stopped.

'*Traitor?*' he snapped. And nodded when he saw her expression.

He sank wearily on to the chair, as though too exhausted to care that she was still standing.

He began, 'I hoped to win your trust through my behaviour. There are, indeed, rumours about me that would make any man shun my company.'

'I know,' she murmured.

'Now, yes, since the Laird accused me.'

She was shaking her head, determined now to tell him everything. 'I had a message from my father, when we were setting out.'

'When your fiancé rode after us?'

She nodded. 'Father said that you'd been expelled from Portugal during Napoleon's first campaign.'

'And?'

'There's not much more.' She found her father's note and handed it to him.

'I see. And now you've heard me called a traitor you imagine it all fits together.'

'And doesn't it? You leave London suddenly, hastening north as though enemies were hounding you. Your old friends turn you out . . .'

'And new friends doubt, before they know me.'

Startled that her opinion could so disturb him, Georgina glanced at him. He was scowling, but *why?*

She felt distressed, as though she were somehow failing him by her lack of faith.

'I wish you would tell me what you were doing in Portugal,' she said quietly, 'so I can understand. I'd be happy to believe you.'

'Believe? No, it's proof you want. And trust that I need.'

Georgina sat on a hard chair, wondering if she dared sleep.

Despite her confusion, she must have dozed. She wakened with a start and in the moonlight saw Howard gazing towards her, his expression bemused, a faint smile on his lips.

'Yes?' she enquired.

'I was simply . . . thinking.'

'And?'

He took a long time over replying.

'It is nothing. A fanciful night-thought.'

'Tell me, nevertheless.'

'Reflecting, it seemed I had won your trust already, if only briefly. Or your father's note would have sent you scuttling home to Kent . . .'

She inhaled deeply. 'Instead of which I am

with you in Scotland,' she stated, understanding as she said the words that returning to Kent would be an admission of failure. And how could she bear to leave him? 'I haven't given up yet.'

'But will you? Will you run home to your family?'

'I am not turning back now. I'll do anything to keep this chance of furthering my career.'

'Then we must protect you.'

'Protect?'

'You're not a child, Georgina. You must be aware of the dangers facing any young attractive woman. You heard the innkeeper, here, you know what he believed. And any man, seeing you travelling unchaperoned, will assume that you'd not discourage attentions.'

Confused, she shook her head. 'I don't understand.'

'No? Lord above, you'd risk rape again before you'll hear reason!'

'But what can you do?'

'I'm the one you're travelling with so, what could be simpler? I become your protection.'

'How do you mean?'

'With a ring on your finger, and me at your side, who'd dare make attempt on your virtue?'

'A ring?'

'A marriage band,' he snapped. 'What else? We're no distance from Gretna. We'll be wed — after that I'll see no man touches you.'

'Marriage?' Georgina was incredulous.

'In name. For the sake of your career.'

'Father would never consent,' she murmured.

'What's changed you, that suddenly you must consult him concerning your future?'

'I . . . you forget, I'm betrothed.'

Howard appeared exasperated, and closed his eyes. 'The arrangement need not be permanent.'

'You treat matrimony very lightly!'

'That's not so. How would *you* ensure that no one molests you?'

'I . . . I . . .'

'You can't answer me! How will you hope to look after yourself? And how secure is lodging when you're called a wanton again and shown the door?'

'There must be a way . . .'

'There are two — one to Kent, the other to Gretna.'

The smithy was dark except for the glow from its fire, for it was evening by the time they reached Gretna and found the blacksmith who would wed them. Wearied by travelling and full of apprehension Georgina felt as though she were in a dream.

Howard murmured to the blacksmith over in a corner. She heard the chink of coins, but it all seemed unreal. She glanced down at her gown, which was wet at the hem from slush and creased from sitting. This could not be her wedding day, not when she felt so desolate. With neither friends nor family to wish her well, no one even to care that she looked so dreadful.

The heat from the forge was so intense after the frost outside that she was afraid she might faint before the business was concluded. And would that really matter? How could she even pretend to play such a part?

Howard was walking towards her; blue eyes, dark in the light of the flames, seeking her gaze with hypnotic intensity.

She had felt before that he mesmerized her. Surely now there could be no other explanation of her acceptance of all this. Of her acceptance of him.

The blacksmith was speaking swiftly, the accent so strong that she could not even understand. Georgina swallowed hard, what a travesty this was of what a marriage should be!

Howard's voice, firm and familiar, startled her into glancing from her restless hands to his face. His gaze seemed locked on to her, and some trick of the flickering light would have had her believing that he truly cared. That could not be. Hadn't he said that the marriage was but a giving of a ring that would protect her from being molested. And hadn't the very coldness of his making all arrangements left her feeling utterly isolated. A puppet. Even now, she seemed so far away that the words Howard was saying made no sense. And those that she uttered in response were a meaningless repetition of the blacksmith's prompting.

Suddenly the atmosphere changed. Howard and the old man were looking to her, expecting some response; confused, she made herself concentrate. Her hand — that was what they wanted. Obediently, she extended shaking fingers over the anvil.

Howard's grasp was sure on hers, warm, as he slid the glinting ring on to her finger. She could have believed, just for the moment, that he meant the promises he was making. Were any of this real . . .

And then the blacksmith was speaking to him, chuckling, and before she was aware of his intentions Howard was pulling her to him. His arms were strong about her so that, grateful that she no longer felt that awful solitude, she looked up.

His lips met hers fiercely, as if to assert

possession of her. It was no token kiss. Parting her lips, his tongue probed while his mouth moved over hers as though he would compel some response. And she wasn't unaffected — gathered into his strength, all her desolation became just a memory. Thankfully, her own lips stirred beneath his kiss, and she felt his arms tighten around her.

They stopped at a wayside cottage when it seemed they would find nowhere to stay.

'We are travellers seeking shelter,' Howard began, when an old man opened the door. 'Could you perhaps accommodate us for the night?'

'This is no inn,' the man snapped.

'I'm aware of that, I thought maybe . . . Is there an inn close by then?'

'Close? There's no habitation for twenty miles around.'

'As I feared. My wife is exhausted, and . . .'

'You'd best step inside.' Grudgingly, the man moved aside to admit them to a combined kitchen and living room. A cruzie provided the only light. Its powerful smell gave ample evidence that it was the receptacle for the frying pan's residue.

'The wife's abed this past hour, it's late for travellers.'

'I know, I know,' Howard agreed.

'There's but one room spare.'

Georgina gazed anxiously towards her employer.

'We'll take the room, and thank you,' Howard asserted, and quelled her with a glare. He called the coachman to bring their possessions.

'Follow me then.' Lighting a candle, the owner of the cottage led the way up bare stone steps to a sparsely furnished room beneath low eaves.

'You cannot expect me to spend the night in here with you,' Georgina exclaimed the moment the door was closed upon their reluctant host.

'This is the very reason we were wed,' Howard snapped. 'But if you prefer the carriage you know where it stands.' He crossed to the uncurtained window. 'You'll be left alone there. Our coachman is being taken to a barn.'

She gazed towards the bed which, although plainly covered, appeared comfortable. 'You could have given me the room for myself. There's no one to molest me here.'

She stood indecisively near the middle of the room. Supposing she chose to sleep in the carriage; could she not manage to drive off? With the moon lighting the road, she could perhaps reach the nearest town by daylight.

Howard turned from the window. 'You may as well sleep, even the horses have been led off to a stall.'

He might have known his statement had dismissed all hope, his expression was so amused.

'You appeared tired earlier, in need of a bed . . .'

'And if I was?'

'You were the one determined to travel, and yet you're easily put about by discomfort!'

He was mocking her: playing some game, the keen blue gaze never leaving her. She sensed that her quickened breathing had drawn his attention to her rising breasts. She drew her pelisse about her, and turned away her head.

'Georgina . . .' His gentle tone surprised her into facing him again.

He extended both hands towards her yet made no other move. Only his eyes betrayed an excitement that matched the thudding of her own pulses.

Why was it that, so unsuitably paired, they aroused in each other a response fierce as lightning?

Georgina realized suddenly that much as she might fear this man, he was now her husband. If she ran away he could fetch her back; if he wished, he could make her his to-night.

Excitement tremored through her again, and though she willed it to stop the feeling grew. Her traitorous body clamoured to be one with him. But still she tried to ignore him.

'You'll surely remove the pelisse, your gown as well,' Howard said coolly, turning from her. 'I've no intention of spending money on replacing garments you've neglected.'

Glaring over her shoulder, a retort ready, she froze. Howard had removed coat and waistcoat already and was unfastening his breeches. She swallowed hard, and closed her eyes only to open them again lest he surprise her, by crossing to embrace her.

'Protection was what I promised,' he reminded her, revealing that he recognized one cause at least of her reluctance to undress. She went to her baggage, found her nightgown and began swiftly to remove her coat and dress. If she moved quickly she could be between the sheets before she could think.

She did not glance towards him again until she was wearing her nightgown. And now, it seemed, his powerful blue eyes sought her entirely. They appeared dark as they'd been in the smithy at Gretna, and boring through her to her very soul. It would have been so easy to rush towards him.

Howard willed his breathing to slow. Only a moment before he'd reiterated his promise of protection. How could he win her trust if he allowed himself to even contemplate taking her as his wife? Lord, she was beautiful, though; a girl who sent the blood surging through his veins.

Her nightgown revealed the curve of her shoulder, gleaming white in the candlelight, beckoning his touch, reminding him of the glimpse he'd had of firm breasts which seemed to beg caresses of him. How in the world had he imagined that he might sleep beside this lovely creature and deny himself? Had he no more sense than a mere lad who'd never experienced passion's demands? Or had he dulled all reasoning because he'd believed he must give her his name?

His wife, though — *his*. And his fault it was that she appeared so apprehensive of him. He walked towards her, his sole intention reassurance. His hand went to her shoulder. The feel of her skin, softer than velvet, seemed to obliterate sense in a tide of sensation. He heard her tiny gasp but, conscious of no protest, pulled her to him. Her hair had been loosened to tumble in a silken cascade. It seemed to caress his hands as they travelled over the thin material of her nightgown while he drew her to his hard body.

As he approached, Georgina had glanced from his eyes to the broad shoulders that offered welcome strength, and, she'd felt the assurance she'd experienced at Gretna returning.

No past event had initiated her in the mysteries of a gentleman's sleeping attire, but she quickly understood that this man wore little beneath his nightshirt. Through his thin garment and her own, she felt him taut against her, pressing into her as if demanding closer contact. His chest invited further pressure from breasts suddenly alive with a delicious tingling, and thighs hot against hers urged that flesh dissolve and remove all barriers.

She stirred against him, feeling now no fear, only an intense longing to have the marriage that had seemed so strange become true marriage. She raised her face, eyes closed, and felt his breath on her eyelids as his lips claimed her own. His kiss was fierce, his lips were brutal as they crushed hers passionately, and his tongue excited her as he savoured the moisture beyond her parting teeth. Some feeling deep within asserted there was nothing to fear in this man who was now her husband.

Her own body was thrusting against him, thigh slithering over thigh. Her hands linked behind him, low down on his spine, so that they stood as one, closely intertwined.

Georgina shivered as his arms dropped away from her. She felt his fingers gently yet surely loosening her clasped hands, as he ended their kiss.

'You said you were tired,' he said sharply. 'We're here to sleep.'

He wanted the whole of her; he'd not take her like this, while her ripe young body showed an eagerness she could later regret.

Trying to still her trembling limbs, Georgina went to the bed to lay there, rigid, as far away from him as possible. He need not have reminded her so cruelly that Virginia Mayburn was the only woman he wanted — that this marriage was as meaningless as the cheap brass ring cold upon her finger.

CHAPTER FIVE

Georgina was thankful when commencing work gave her a distraction from Howard's behaviour. She might accept that he could not explain away the accusations, but was less ready to acknowledge that he'd no wish to claim her as his wife. The wintry Lowlands held their own sorcery, however, entrancing her to sketch on, oblivious of the cold, until numbed fingers had to be stuffed inside her muff.

Some days Howard walked alone, more often he sat with her, reading from his manuscript, so that she learned to see great house and castle, loch and towering ben, with his writer's eye. And to admire a fellow craftsman.

Happiness lent a sparkle to Georgina's dark eyes. Howard noticed how this complemented the colour stung to her cheeks by the wind, and frequently checked the hand that would have caressed that bloom. He had forbidden himself all contact with her skin, their new intimacy had revealed his susceptibility. Most nights he retired to their stark room with an ache that had grown during an evening spent sitting with her on either side of the inn's hearth. Elsewhere, he'd have gone to the town's easy women. Here, he could think only of the girl whose dark hair brushed his cheek on the pillow, longing for her when, in sleep, she curved unwittingly against him. And although their being the only guests had relaxed his wariness, this new tension seemed the harder.

He reminded himself that she had married him solely for her career, that her determination had made her deceive her way into his employment. Geo. Morton, indeed! He often wished she were a man. He wouldn't be consumed then by this great pulsating itch that knew no appeasement.

And then their work here was ended. Georgina longed for Howard to praise her skill. She had watched his sharp blue eyes scanning her illustrations and the approving nod which often accompanied his scrutiny. His mood, however, seemed as dour as the grey skies that hung low over the hills.

'So, we shall be travelling home before long,' she remarked, expecting he'd express satisfaction that the task was completed quickly.

He nodded. 'Yes. And a wearisome journey lies ahead of us.'

'Do you intend that we visit the Mallaigs again?'

'I imagine so.'

'You don't sound particularly interested.'

He shrugged, toying with a fork. 'I know only that I shall be thankful when we reach London.'

Recalling Lady Virginia Mayburn's beauty she knew how she dreaded having him disregard their marriage in favour of his cousin. But she had to ask the question.

'Perhaps there is someone from whom you have been too long absent?'

'Oh? Whom do you suppose?'

'Lady Virginia, of course.'

Startled, he regarded her curiously. 'And why should you imagine that I am in any haste to return to her?'

'Surely you and she . . .' She left the sentence unfinished.

'You are making assumptions that all too often have been made by others. Granted, my cousin is extremely attractive. She is also in a position to offer me a home when I am in London. Neither of us care for speculation regarding our relationship.'

As they prepared for their long journey home and he appeared increasingly anxious to have it concluded, Georgina became ever more certain that his words had been calculated to distract her. He had said nothing about their marriage being made known to her family or his own. He must want simply to be rid of her.

The snow had ceased falling as they headed south and rain made travelling uncomfortable. The upholstery of the carriage felt damp, adding to Georgina's misery.

She sat dejectedly in her corner, scarcely noticing the scenery beyond the rivulets chasing down the window, and wishing that Howard might have just one word of encouragement for her, if only about her drawings.

They were a few miles short of the border when a sudden jolting shook each of them from their silent thoughts. The horse had slithered on a patch of ice and one of the carriage wheels had been damaged against a milestone.

'The trouble is not severe, sir,' said the coachman, 'but I fear we must stop at the wheelwright's in the next village.'

'Oh, really!' Howard exclaimed, exasperated. 'Is everything contriving to delay us!'

He was clearly in an ill humour when they halted. He hardly spoke at all to Georgina although they had found an inn offering refreshment. He glanced uneasily about as though he couldn't abide the place. Yet she was finding the glowing open fire and cheerful conversation all around them a welcome respite.

Howard hastily drained his glass and rose.

'Remain where you are if you will. I must ensure that the wheelwright doesn't take all day over the repair.'

Georgina gazed about the crowded tables, catching snatches of conversation in the lilting Scots that she found so difficult.

She took out her sketching pad, for she enjoyed attempting caricature. Intent on capturing the energy of one drover's face, she didn't notice two men slipping on to the bench on either side of her.

'Begging your pardon, ma'am,' one fellow began. 'But we were interested, seeing you draw. It is rare to find a young lady who is so accomplished.'

Flattered, Georgina smiled.

'Oh, I'm not very skilled — houses and landscapes are more my . . .'

'Oh yes, ma'am, we know,' the other man remarked. 'Being as how you're working with Mr Saunders.'

'You know him!' she exclaimed, pleased to meet, so far from London, friends of Howard.

'We know who he is, yes. And that you have been visiting the Lowlands.'

'We stayed there while I illustrated his latest book.' She frowned. 'But I don't understand what you want . . .'

'There's no need for you to understand, ma'am,' one man interrupted. 'All we want to know is where he's heading now . . .'

'Miss Morton!'

Howard's enraged shout had everyone in the inn turning to the door. Instinctively, Georgina rose, which was as well for he strode across and dragged her from the table as though he would tear her arm from its socket.

'Let me be!' she hissed, even more upset because he'd used her maiden name.

His grasp like a vice, he pulled her through the door, then hauled her along the road to the carriage. He thrust her inside then followed, slamming the door.

'Drive on,' he shouted to their coachman and then he faced her, his eyes grim.

'Have you no more sense than to speak with common travellers, and about my business!'

'I was not, I . . .'

'I heard you, madam. It may satisfy you to learn that you have most likely placed your own life in grave danger along with mine.'

'Surely not. They were only asking about my work . . .'

'Your work, my . . . !' He drew in a deep shuddering breath. 'Good God, woman, haven't I problems enough without being cursed by your stupidity!'

'But they were only . . .'

He interrupted, 'Did they mention my name?'

'Yes, but . . .'

'As I thought! And they enquired, no doubt, if we were en route for London.'

'Well . . .'

'Well,' he cried, 'well! Thanks to your careless tongue, the possibility that anything for me will ever again be *well* grows increasingly remote!'

'But I do not understand.'

'Of course you don't. You're a witless female!'

'You are upset,' Georgina said, her tone quiet. 'And I will try to excuse your abuse.'

'Upset,' he shouted. 'Indeed not! I am angry! Angry that you could so lightly inform those who would harm me.'

'Harm?'

'Seize, execute . . .' He paused. 'We must change our plans. We will avoid Carlisle, take a different route. And pray God the start we have on those two be sufficient . . .'

They reached an inn after jolting through desolate countryside at a breath-taking pace. Howard sat silently throughout, so taut that Georgina didn't dare speak.

Now she was determined to have some explanation.

'What have you done, Howard?'

He glanced from the meal for which he obviously had no appetite and looked at her across the table. He sighed but did not answer.

'Why are we fleeing as though you were a common criminal?'

'Perhaps that is what I am,' he suggested bitterly, 'maybe that is why no one, least of all you, will accept my word.'

Georgina set aside knife and fork. 'Howard,' she began, and wondered how long she had used his Christian name. 'Howard, did this trouble begin in Portugal?'

'You're no more prepared to trust me than if I were some stranger that you'd met only this afternoon.'

'You're wrong. Must I remind you that I've placed my own safety entirely in your hands? But I am not — as you seem to hope — an unthinking idiot who does not question behaviour that is bewildering and frightening. What have you done?'

'The nature of my commission in Portugal must remain secret,' he said, his tone flat and inflexible.

Feeling defeated, she rose, but before she could turn away from the table, he continued.

'It is no fault of mine that my motives were misinterpreted.'

She realized suddenly that he needed her unquestioning compliance. 'Forget that I troubled you with questions, I promise I'll ask no more.'

'Yes,' he responded gravely. 'I do regret, Georgina, that involvement with me endangers you. Believe that, and forgive me when the increased responsibility darkens my mood.'

Smiling, she touched his arm. 'Relax tonight. We'll face tomorrow together.'

His lips curved slightly, even the blue eyes appeared warmer. 'You have not quite decided then to quit my company?'

Georgina smiled. 'You seem alert enough to all danger. I'd travel with no one else!'

Despite her light words, Georgina could not rest easily that night and lay staring into the darkness of their room, wondering what could have brought about Howard's expulsion from the Peninsular. And why he was pursued in his own country.

Towards dawn she wakened from a fitful sleep, disturbed by some sound. Howard was silhouetted against the window, motionless, staring into the night as though gravely perturbed. And she could not have him bear the problems alone. She was his wife, if only in name. And now she saw today as if it were inevitable journey's end, bringing too soon — much too soon — the parting that she'd no wish for. In sharing so great a part of Howard's life she had felt her tenderness towards him ever increasing. Feeling him warm beside her in the bed, she had known the pleasures of an intimacy that instilled comfort though it denied union. In the daytime she had admired his smartly-clad shoulders, conscious of her familiarity with their breadth, and the thrill when he discarded his shirt on undressing. And she recognized that her interest in him was close to love.

Leaving the bed, she crossed quietly to join him.

Howard started as she reached his side. He frowned, but did not disengage her arm when she slipped it through his. For several moments he said nothing, then he faced her. 'So, I have disturbed you.'

He meant that he had wakened her. But her disturbance was so much more powerful than the absence of sleep. As her arm had linked with his a current strong enough to make her giddy passed between them. She swallowed, trying to steady her rocketing pulse.

'I am young enough to take no harm from losing a little sleep.'

'And too young for sharing my unrest.'

'I'm not a child.'

He was searching her face, as if he savoured the features, etching them on his memory.

'Indeed, Georgina, I'm well aware of your maturity.'

Briefly, he closed his eyes, trying to still his emotions. That she had joined him when he longed for her, was turmoil. To have her nearness engender this sweet-sharp desire was unbearable.

'Go back to bed.'

Shaking her head, she smiled up at him. 'Is it better that I should lie awake alone whilst you, equally restless, should stand here?'

'Wiser,' he stated, before caution silenced him.

The mullioned window gave a view across moorland, still snow-covered despite the rain. Stars freckled the cobalt sky and a faint paling at the horizon augured of dawn's approach.

Feeling the chill off the glass, Georgina moved instinctively nearer to him. His arm encircled her and again he gazed into her face. How brilliant her eyes were, so clear. With such a girl as mate, a man should withstand anything. And if accepting her allegiance placed her in jeopardy? Would reckoning her protection his privilege justify such a risk?

Howard sighed. He knew he'd not be able to excuse himself any indulgence. But for the present she was here, so close that her nightgown fluttered at his bare ankles; while the pulsing of her heart against his side echoed the more urgent throbbing in his loins. God, here was temptation! But how, he demanded silently, how despatch her alone to bed — when he would press himself into the warmth that would appease anxiety and desire alike?

He checked a moan, permitting his eyes alone to feast on this creature who'd enraptured him since their first meeting.

The light of early morning illumined the twin breasts gleaming at her low-cut bodice. He tightened the arms encircling her to prevent his fingers straying to trace the enticing curve. And still it seemed the touch of peach-textured skin tingled through. Fearing she might be conscious of his passion, he glanced again to her eyes. And saw there a longing that equalled his own.

If only he had a home to give this lovely girl, *his wife*. What a fool he'd been to let anything prevent him settling the debt to his cousin. What mattered work now, when but a day or so and Georgina would be gone for ever. How would he live alone, when he'd come this close to living with her?

The madness which had incited him to suggest their marriage had become his punishment, flaring into a frustration that seemed never ending. He glanced again to her face, and discovered tears on her dark lashes. He drew her to him. Again, Georgina learned how slightly fine fabric disguised sensation. Exciting her so that she forgot her distress. He was hard against her, his body taut, masterful. His kiss seemed to assert that troubled he might be, diminished never.

She revelled in the strength of the arms that held her so firmly against his chest, crushing her breasts with a ferocity to match the force that threatened to burn away the flesh keeping his hardness from her. If only she might be possessed by his strength she'd feel secure for ever.

His mouth was moving over hers, demanding as the hands that fondled her body, his probing tongue exciting her further so that she moved ceaselessly against him, aware of the swiftness of his breath and her own, and rejoicing in his desire for her.

His fingers were at the fastening of her nightgown, then caressing her naked breasts until she felt she would cry out for more, to have his touch win from her even greater delights. And then he was carrying her to the bed, snatching off her nightgown and gazing at her, before tossing aside his own garment and lying beside her.

He cupped her breast, fondling as her nipple hardened beneath his fingers, while his other hand stroked the inside of her thigh, travelling upwards, arousing her to such delight that nothing could have induced her to remain still. And then he found her hand, taking her fingers to the curling hair at his chest and then down over his taut belly.

Georgina gasped, thrilled to learn the strength of his desire and wishing both to prolong this magical excitement and have it satisfied. The thighs that had parted for his exploring hands trembled, echoing the pulsating in her loins, and she marvelled that so exquisite a sensation could insist that further ecstasy be hers.

And now Howard's lips were at her breasts, his tongue alerting from her fresh responses before they travelled upwards to her throat. Placing butterfly kisses on chin then cheeks, he kissed her ear, nibbling at its lobe, and then he found her mouth once more. And as his tongue darted between her teeth he eased her on to her back, following her, hip against hip, thigh touching thigh. His chest seemed to caress her breasts and he was firm, urgent, against her. She felt herself arching to him, longing to assure him of her welcome; and then he was hard between her thighs, probing as though he would be gentle, yet pressing so strongly as he entered that she cried out.

'I'd not hurt you,' he murmured, as though the power thrusting into her were stronger than his will.

'Oh, Howard,' she gasped and then again; 'oh!' as she felt him moving, pushing, as if he would draw even closer inside her. Her arms were about his strong shoulders, her lips clinging to his as she held on to him with her entire body. Together they moved, arousing new sensations, fresh excitements, until at last their urgency rose in one great crescendo to leave her weak but blissfully contented.

Howard's lips were upon her cheek again, and on her neck, soft drowsy kisses as, passion sated, his breathing quietened. Georgina felt joy envelop her; if this was being loved then she knew nothing remotely to compare with its fulfilment. The weeks might have seemed long while she had waited to become his wife, but she regretted no second of the time now it had won her this exultation. She was his now, because he wanted and needed her. Out of all the world she was the one he'd chosen.

His steady breathing told her that now he slept. And the dawn revealed the line of the firm shoulders that had held her to him. His hair, darkened by moisture from the heat they'd kindled, curled over his forehead. His cheeks were flushed still. Georgina controlled the impulse to stroke the long fair eyelashes lest she wake him. She too must sleep. Time there'd be, often enough, for further rejoicing in this fine man who had made himself hers.

When she awakened, though, she was alone. Could it be that Howard already regretted the passion that had made her his?

CHAPTER SIX

Howard was at breakfast, and greeted her with a reserve that sent her spirits plunging further. Georgina had to force food between her reluctant lips. How could she pretend to be other than distressed when this cold stranger was the man who had taught her only hours before that loving him was far more important than her career. She could scarcely believe now that this was her husband, and that his grave features concealed a passion that had soared exultant with her own. Could he not have let her believe, if only for today, that she mattered to him?

Once they had set out, however, he became less remote, allowing no more than his customary wariness to distract him from sharing with her his interest in the countryside. They stopped at Castle Howard and her eyes widened as she gazed about, to the sun glinting off snow-covered gardens and the splendid house.

A hand on her shoulder, Howard turned her to face the long terrace extending from the house to the Temple of the Four Winds.

'Is there time to make a drawing?' Georgina asked.

'If you're as swift as you were working for me. But the drawings may not be utilized. I've written nothing about Castle Howard.'

'Perhaps you should,' she smiled; 'to accompany my illustrations.'

Quelling an impulse to embrace this provocative creature, Howard lowered his arm from her shoulders. Lord, the irony of learning how well she might match him, when all she cared for was her career. Any future explorations he undertook would seem so dull, and solitary.

His subdued manner when they settled again into the carriage, escaped her notice. She chattered on about the hilly countryside, asking that he show her on the map just where Castle Howard was situated.

The map that he produced from amongst his papers was one that he himself had drawn.

'Let me examine this closely,' she begged. 'You draw maps superbly. You must find the ability very . . . profitable.'

He snatched the paper from her, slipping it away from sight before she had even glimpsed where Castle Howard lay. His expression grim, his cheeks flaring, he stared from the window.

Georgina wondered why her innocent remark had made him so ill-tempered. They were near the end of the day before she managed to rouse him.

She knew that Howard was interested in the improvement of roads throughout the kingdom, and had read his account of the Turnpike Trusts. She'd seen for herself the turning stiles, spiked to prevent passage of those who would evade the toll, and listened when he described a splendid bridge being constructed under Telford's supervision at Dunkeld in the Highlands.

In an effort to interest him, she remarked upon the smoother surface of their road. 'Was this made by Telford perhaps?'

'I believe not,' Howard stated coolly, reluctantly ending his preoccupation with the distance.

'How can you know?' she prompted.

'I find out all I can about the routes I encourage others to travel.'

'I know — and that you're most thorough in everything you attempt.'

The blue gaze appeared to assess her for signs of a mere wish to flatter. Evidently satisfied, he crossed one long slender leg over the other.

'This stretch of road owes its existence to a remarkable man. Born John Metcalf, he was blinded when but a lad . . .'

'Blinded?' she gasped, 'then how did he construct roads?'

'Blind Jack of Knaresborough, as he became known, was a man to admire. He continued with sports, fought at Culloden . . .'

'He couldn't have . . .'

'You'll not argue with me over one who's long been my hero.' Enthusiasm had replaced irritation, warming his tone. 'Blind Jack was contracted to build a Turnpike between Harrogate and Boroughbridge, not all that far from here. His recognition of the need for staunch foundations and efficient drainage won him more and more work.'

'Proof that determination overcomes a deal of obstacles.'

'You'll appreciate that,' Howard said in a rare admission of approval.

Cheered by this hitherto unrevealed glimpse of her husband Georgina reflected on the fact that *he* approved such qualities. How could anyone suppose such a man capable of deceit?

In York they halted for a night to return the carriage they had been loaned. Georgina had believed Howard would take her with him, but she was to remain curious about his acquaintance for he left her behind at the inn. And although they shared a room he seemed reluctant to even touch her.

Their journey from York to London was to be by mail coach so their route could not be varied. Howard became watchful again of all their fellow travellers and of those they met whenever the coach stopped.

Georgina longed for him to confide his reasons for dreading arrest. Nothing seemed to brighten his countenance.

She laughed and applauded with the rest when one of the coach's guards produced a bugle and from it a lilting tune for their amusement, but Howard remained un-smiling even when he tossed coins from his pocket into the fellow's hat.

Nearing London on the last day, the snow which had fallen intermittently was re-placed by fog, so that they arrived late at the inn which was to be their terminus.

'You'll not reach Sevenoaks comfortably tonight,' Howard told her flatly. 'But I imagine we can accommodate you with a bed.'

His expression was inscrutable. She felt torn — any extension of his company was welcome, yet she was reluctant to visit the house in Grosvenor Place since learning it was owned by his cousin.

Lady Virginia's ecstatic greeting of Howard sent Georgina's heart to the sole of her slippers. How could she have imagined that he might, after all, tell his cousin of their marriage? Since that one blissful night he had not even embraced her. And had suggested that very morning that there was no further need for her to wear the brass ring. When Georgina was given into the charge of Mrs Veryan, the housekeeper, she felt miserably that she was being taught her position in this house.

Her room was pleasant, nonetheless, and Mrs Veryan too conscious of etiquette to be other than polite. But it was with a leaden heart that Georgina joined Howard and Virginia for dinner in the room dominated by an exquisitely polished table resplendent with fine silverware and delicate china.

Howard told his cousin of their travels, drawing Georgina into the conversation, but always the assured red-head managed to turn the discussion to other matters. Georgina could scarcely feel sorry when her final evening with the man who had become her husband was ended.

They were to make an early start next morning, using his cousin's Berlin again. Georgina was surprised when she heard someone moving about the corridor some long while after midnight.

She heard a rapping which seemed to be

on her door and, thrusting on her robe, she went eagerly to open it. The knocking was upon the door next to her own and a silken-robed figure was slipping through into its discreetly lighted interior.

'Howard . . .' Lady Virginia began as she disappeared from view.

Georgina waited to hear no more.

Gulping down her distress, she quietly closed her own door. Dejectedly, she sank on to the bed, wondering already if the arms that had held her so close now extended for Lady Virginia. And if they did, she told herself, who was she to condemn? She had agreed to marriage in name only; had been, at first, reluctant to consummate the union. And here was the moment that she'd dreaded, when she must dismiss all dreams of pairing with a man whose interests matched her own, whose artistry with words painted pictures, whose body had taught her the wonders of loving. Because the desire he experienced was for his cousin.

Disturbed by longing, and by her own fancies of what might be happening beyond the wall, Georgina missed the click of a latch which could have reassured her. And so she did not sleep in that strange bed from which she tumbled eventually with heavy eyes.

Disappointment was a solid lump at the

pit of her stomach. She would learn to live with the reality of Howard's affection for Lady Virginia, but couldn't she have been left *something?* Her career also appeared to be ended now. Howard had been careful to express no enthusiasm for her work, and had kept his future plans from her.

Overnight the fog had cleared, giving fine weather to ensure a swift journey to Sevenoaks. It was long enough, however, for Georgina to sense the silence of the man accompanying her, and to assume he had already dismissed her. Doubtless, he was contemplating living in seclusion with that red-haired beauty.

The absence of conversation unnerved her so that as he handed her from the carriage she was compelled to comment.

'You are very quiet.'

'Did you expect then that, today, I would be frivolous!' The blue eyes scrutinized her as though her lack of comprehension bewildered him. He seemed pained and she would have asked the reason but it was no use. Already her mother, who'd been advised of her return, was rushing out to greet her.

Although Mrs Morton had thawed sufficiently to welcome Howard, the ensuing half-hour proved awkward.

Roland was there and the warmth of his embrace embarrassed Georgina before this man who was her husband. Only Nannie Meg with her accustomed hug made her feel easy, and pleased her also by thrusting a gnarled hand into Howard's palm.

'You've cared well for the lassie,' she approved. 'I read that in the assurance of her step. She'll have learned from her experiences and that harms nobody.'

It was as Georgina walked to the door when Howard was departing that Roland caught sight of her bare finger.

'Georgina,' he exclaimed in horror, 'my ring — why are you not wearing it?'

Aghast, she wondered how she had so readily overlooked it that she was unprepared with excuses for its loss.

'I . . .' Lost, she glanced for help to Howard.

Smiling easily, he gazed down at her. 'Oh, Georgina — your ring! In your haste to be home we have quite neglected it!' He turned to Roland. 'Throughout our journeying, Mr Crowbrook, Miss Morton has been most concerned for your ring's safety. Last evening, therefore, she insisted that I lock it away. Today, alas, she thought of nothing so much as seeing you again.'

Roland seemed mollified. Georgina continued outside with Howard.

'Thank you for making my excuses,' she said as he paused beside the carriage step. 'But why did you?'

'My dear Georgina, you alone can decide if your relationship with Mr Crowbrook is to continue. I'll not influence you.'

'But you are my husband . . .'

'For the present.'

Georgina sighed, her heart plummeting as she realized how impossible it was that they'd ever have a real marriage. 'For the present', he had said, as though he would be rid of her before she could protest. Already it was too late, his hand was at the carriage door. But she could not bear to have him go while she knew nothing of his plans not where he would be.

'Where will you go next?' she enquired. 'Where next would you — you guide those who read your books?'

The quaver in her voice gave him hope that more than curiosity prompted her question. 'Tuscany,' he told her quickly, 'I am collating information on Florence. Later, I go on to Rome.'

'I see,' she said flatly.

'But travelling so far does not attract you?'

'I don't understand . . .'

'I'll need an artist still you know. There's

no time to find another.'

'You mean . . . ?' Wonder enlarged her dark eyes which misted with tears. Maybe he did care for her, after all.

Howard raised an eyebrow. 'Or are you daunted perhaps by what you've experienced with me of late?'

Georgina's delight was soon submerged in her mother's disapproval, which was reinforced when her father, summoned from his barracks, arrived.

His expression was grave. 'I must speak with you at once, Georgina.'

He indicated that she could sit but he remained standing at the window of his study, a tall figure, distinguished in the officer's uniform, his light-coloured hair reminding her of Howard.

'Your mother has informed me of your intention, and rightly so.'

'No one approved of my working,' Georgina said quietly; 'I cannot expect that you should . . .'

Her father frowned. 'My objection is not to the principle of your taking paid employment, though Lord knows there's no need of that with young Crowbrook offering for you. No, Georgina, my concern is on different grounds. You had my note, and know therefore something of Howard Saunders' history. I foresee more fighting in the Peninsular — when that occurs this unpleasant business may well be resurrected.'

Georgina said nothing. She had heard the suspicions often enough. And had decided to judge Howard only on his behaviour towards herself.

'I am conscious that Mr Saunders is suspected of some misdemeanour.'

'Is that how you call it? Well, I'll name him a French spy.'

When she had sat during several laboured minutes without comment, her father faced her, leaning his hands on the desk and forcing his features close to her own. 'What say you now, miss?'

'Are you forbidding me to take this journey to Florence?'

'That is not my way, as I believe you are aware. You are sufficiently mature to know when you should be taking my advice.'

'Then I am sorry for grieving you and Mother, but in this matter I feel better equipped to know Howard Saunders for the kind of man he is.'

'Then be ever watchful and alert,' her father said before leaving the study. 'And remember that I taught you to take care of yourself. We can only pray some intervention prevents further trouble.'

Something in her father's tone implied that he was not revealing his own intentions. Could it be that he knew enough about Howard to have him brought before a magistrate? Or whoever judged those suspected of treason abroad. She could not bear the thought that her own father might be responsible for the arrest of the man she had married.

Before preparing to meet Roland that evening, she wrote Howard a note:

Since you did not intimate how soon we should be embarking on our next journey, I am enquiring when our departure might be. My father has expressed concern. There could be some preventive measure.

Sealing the missive and hurrying to catch the mail, it occurred to her that Howard might now cancel the proposed visit to Florence, and deny her reason for seeing him.

She sighed. Ah well, better that than he be deprived of freedom. Or worse.

Roland greeted her warmly that evening. He took her to his uncle's offices in High Street.

Georgina had not previously visited the suite of rooms where her fiancé worked, and she exclaimed now on the good taste of their furnishings. Roland smiled at her approval but seemed in great haste to begin discussing their marriage plans. When he'd suggested bringing her here for that purpose she had decided she must tell him quickly, that she was married already. And if he refused to keep this from her family then she must bear their disapproval. Before she could speak, however, Roland drew her to him, kissing her fervently.

'Let us be more comfortable.' He led her through to a room beyond his uncle's office and to a couch. Again, he embraced her, and Georgina realized that discussing matrimony might not have been his sole purpose in bringing her here.

Roland did indeed intend to utilize every second of this evening. Georgina was his fiancée, he'd ensure that she remained in no doubt of that fact. His hands were travelling over her back and shoulders already, his lips moving hungrily over her mouth.

And now those restless hands sought her breasts, caressing, then slipping within her bodice.

'Roland, no,' she protested.

'My love, this is but an introduction, do not remonstrate. When you're my wife there'll be no withholding.'

Before she could speak, his mouth returned to hers, his tongue forcing apart her teeth. She was aware of all the sensations surging through her, creating a powerful vibration that threatened to dull reasoning. Yet this demanding urgency was totally unlike the love she'd felt for Howard. A physical matter, devoid of caring, and inciting in her no desire to give. Was this all there'd ever been between them?

'Roland . . .'

His rapid breathing obliterated her voice and the lips clamped upon her own prevented any protest. To her dismay, her own desire was swiftly aroused, but she recognized its danger.

A warm hand went to her thigh as she struggled to rise. 'No more, Roland.' She was growing frightened. He was no light weight and clearly he had no intention of moving. He seemed not to heed her, and the hand on her leg began easing up her skirt.

'Roland, no!'

'You wear my ring, girl — or would if you'd taken more thought for it. It strikes me you're in my debt for neglecting to wear my token.'

In no doubt now of his purpose, Georgina scrambled to get away from him, but his hand was heavy on her thigh, the greater part of his body resting on her own. He was pinning her to the couch, and he fumbled at the fastening of his breeches while his fingers strayed between her thighs.

Using all her strength, she thrust away his intruding hand and straightened her skirt. But she could not shift him from a position which left her scant chance of breathing, and now she felt moist lips at her throat, and sharp teeth also.

His hand pressed mercilessly at her breast. 'Do not stop me now,' he moaned. 'I could not bear that. I love you so much, I must take you.'

'Take . . . you want to possess me!'

'Eh?' Confused, he leaned away from her a little. Georgina seized the brief chance to slide away.

'Take me home, Roland. Find your coachman and take me home.'

'Forgive me,' he gasped, still breathless.

He continued quite maudlin on the homeward drive, and when she would have ended their engagement by declaring her marriage, caution made her delay that revelation until others could protect her from his anger.

Her father had returned to his regiment and Georgina escaped her mother's disapproval by strolling with Amy and Emily in

Knole Park the next day, and taking them to visit their aunts.

On the second day after her meeting with Roland she was walking alone into town when she was overtaken by a horse-drawn Berlin. It halted a little way ahead.

She smiled brilliantly when Howard stepped from the carriage as she drew level with its door.

He smiled back at her, removing his beaver hat and bowing to her hand which he took in his own. His gaze appeared to scrutinize her features for any change that had occurred during his absence.

'My apologies for giving you no warning, after receiving your message it was wiser for me to leave London. Is your father at home?'

'No. He is gone now.'

He nodded, pensively. 'Come, let's sit in the carriage while we talk. Your message, for which I'm sincerely grateful, has . . .' He hesitated and turned to face her. 'I can only think that you are concerned for me.'

'Of course.'

'But, are you certain that by coming with me in opposition to your family's wishes, you're not risking regrets?'

'I am certain,' Georgina replied calmly, without knowing why she felt so sure.

Again, he smiled. 'Then prepare as swiftly

123

as you can for leaving. Meanwhile I shall wait at a local inn.'

'Perhaps Mother would accommod . . .'

'I think *not*.'

'I am sorry . . .'

'Sorry? Oh, come — when you, Georgina, have proved you've a mind of your own and your own loyalty? The very spirit that irritated me at first has won my admiration . . .'

Amazed, Georgina gazed at him.

'I will return home as soon as I have made my purchases. And I will pack immediately so that we may leave in the morning.'

'Georgina.'

'Yes?'

'Do you trust me?'

'I — I believe so.'

'Would you, without enquiring what they are, accept that there are reasons why I am anxious to make towards Dover before nightfall?'

'If you say that it is so.'

He nodded gravely. 'And would you be prepared to leave secretly, on this occasion, without bidding farewell to everyone?'

Georgina lowered her gaze.

'I would. Only don't you think departing like that might so perturb Mama that she'd send someone to stop us?'

'How well do you trust the old lady —

Nannie Meg, I think you call her?'

'She's been my ally since I was small. Do you want me to confide in her and leave her to explain?'

'Would she?'

'For me, yes.' She sighed, smiling wryly. 'It will be as you ask.'

'Thank you.' Howard's grip tightened on her gloved fingers which had remained in his. Briefly, he also smiled. 'Poor Nannie Meg! You will, I hope, add my thanks to your own.'

They arranged that he would meet her in the garden of her home.

Georgina found Nannie Meg resting in her own small drawing-room.

'What is it now?' the old lady enquired when she came running in to sit beside her footstool. 'You've a flare in those cheeks and a wicked sparkle in your eyes — I'll warrant there's some mischief afoot!'

'Not mischief, dearest Nannie, but a serious scheme which requires your co-operation . . .'

Nannie Meg cast hazel eyes heavenwards. 'Save us the frills then, miss, and be explaining . . . And remember I've promised nothing yet.'

'You know that I am leaving soon for Europe?'

The old lady sniffed. 'The fuss there's been, I should not fall down in surprise if the whole of Sevenoaks was aware of it. But what's troubling you, child?'

'You know how distressed Mama is . . . Well, partly to save her further distress, and . . . let's say for *that* reason — I intend leaving in secret.'

'And I'm the one who's to bear the brunt and tell the poor soul? You are sure, my love, that you know what you're about?'

'You've asked me that before. Now, I am even more certain.'

With Nannie Meg's help, Georgina hurried to join Howard as soon as it grew dark.

His worried expression suggested that he had been waiting some long while. 'You are ready?' he enquired in a whisper. 'Henry — the coachman . . . heard two men enquiring for me at the inn. He had the sense to suggest that I was staying in the vicinity for several days, visiting friends. That should allow us time for getting away from here.'

Georgina gulped. 'Do — do you suppose my father could have sent someone to prevent your leaving the country?'

Howard shrugged. 'I know only that, whoever is behind all this, it increases our urgency — and danger.'

CHAPTER SEVEN

By the time they had reached Dover unchallenged Georgina was beginning to relax; and if Howard remained apprehensive she was far too excited about going abroad to dwell on it.

'How large the ship is!' she exclaimed, but Howard only smiled, and she resolved to say nothing more to remind him how naïve she was. She had been so afraid that he didn't wish her to accompany him. She must show her maturity as a traveller as well as artist.

It was in the sunlight of a crisp February morning that they put out from harbour. Only as the White Cliffs began to recede with the horizon did Howard seem to stand more easily at the rail.

He took her below decks and, when Georgina was seated, settled beside her. He hesitated before speaking. He was looking at the exquisite brown eyes and the slightly parted lips. Lord, how fortunate he was that no one had forbidden her to come, and he vowed that nothing must distract him from keeping her safe. He must quell his own desire, which even at this hour induced the familiar throbbing; and hope that doing so would prove these emotions finer than mere passion. Only in the security of their own room would he allow himself to draw her to him, and then they'd come together in glorious reminder of the strength of their love.

He cleared his throat. 'I think that it will be pleasant making our way slowly towards Florence. This is, I believe, your first visit across the Channel?'

Georgina nodded.

'And there are many places — French châteaux, Alpine villages, of which I've had only a tantalizing glimpse. We'll enjoy exploring them together.'

'Oh, yes.' Her delighted gasp warmed him. He made his tone brisk when he continued.

'Not that I mean work should be neglected. I have notes already of places that I wish to revisit and write up for another guide book. If you can illustrate as swiftly as before, we should keep pace with each other.'

'So when do you expect to reach Tuscany?'

'I haven't decided. I prefer to take whatever time we need en route. Do you mind?'

'Not in the least. I am sure I shall be captivated by the entire journey.'

'Good.'

Georgina smiled. If he continued to consult her on their itinerary, he must indeed consider her an equal.

They continued planning their travels, but Georgina was gradually becoming quite giddy. The motion of the vessel was sending a pulse vibrating through her entire body, and especially in her stomach.

Howard frowned. 'Georgina, are you unwell?'

'It is nothing, a slight giddiness. It will pass.'

She was over-optimistic; the nausea worsened into an attack of sea-sickness so violent that Howard's faint amusement turned to consternation.

For the next interminable hours, Georgina did not know what was going on around her.

And then Howard was rousing her gently.

'The French coast, my dear, we're almost arrived.'

Georgina willed herself to appear composed as they went ashore. Leaning heavily on Howard's arm, she left him to attend to all the formalities.

'You're on firm ground now,' he assured her as they walked along the quayside beside tiny boats bobbing in the harbour. Georgina found his statement difficult to credit. The paving beneath her feet cavorted as though to toss her into the sea. And despite Howard's support, walking a straight course was impossible.

A strong smell of fish rose from nets heaped against a wall, and she breathed deeply to avoid retching. Before they reached the high road where carriages could be hired, she protested that she could walk no further. Her eyes refused to focus properly and hearing faded.

'Georgina!' Howard exclaimed and then: 'Oh, God!' as she swooned.

She recovered consciousness with Howard kneeling at her side. He was loosening her garments at waist and neck.

'Don't,' she protested feebly, 'no . . .' But he continued unfastening her sash and the scarf pinned at her throat.

'Don't you know I'll not harm you,' he said sharply, before his lips twisted wryly. 'Others, it seems, have been less circumspect.'

Georgina could not fathom what had provoked that comment, nor his sudden anger.

He assisted her into the nearest hire carriage. She felt scarcely any better, for jolting over the cobbled streets increased her distress.

They put up at an inn but it was only after

sleeping for several hours that Georgina felt restored, and not until the following morning that she glanced from the tiny window of their room to see the undulating countryside with its farmhouses that looked very different from the Kentish ones familiar to her. The third finger of her left hand was itching, and glancing down, she found a dark stain around the brass band which Howard must have replaced there while she was ill. She slipped the ring from her finger and, when it rolled from the washstand, was about to pick it up when someone rapped on the door.

The maidservant had come with hot water. Quickly, Georgina completed her toilette, observing with embarrassment the purple marks remaining from Roland's impassioned biting at her neck. She knew now what had provoked Howard's angry remark.

He was at the breakfast table already and rose, his blue eyes appraising her for signs of sickness.

'You are recovered.' His words were a statement rather than a query, for he had noticed the brilliance restored to those magnificent brown eyes and the faint rose-flush in the cheeks that he longed even now to touch.

Georgina smiled into his eyes and his heart lurched.

'I am completely well again. And owe you my sincerest thanks for your care.'

'I am relieved that you are none the worse.' His tone was cool, concealing the fury that had raged in him throughout the night. Acutely conscious of Georgina sleeping beside him, he had lain, glaring into the darkness, his concern for her turned swiftly to wrath.

What a fool he had been, he thought now as he watched her consuming a breakfast that would have fortified a farm labourer. What a fool for believing she might care for him. He wasn't so inexperienced that his teeth had never caused dark weals on a woman's throat. He had learned the passion in his wife's exquisite body, and in one glorious night had thought his possession of her would last. Now he'd found how easily she could rush to Crowbrook's embrace. If she no longer wanted *him* as her husband she couldn't have stated her choice more plainly.

'*When* you have finished eating,' he snapped, 'I hope that we may speedily depart.'

'Why, certainly.' She ran still-smiling eyes over his features. 'How far do you plan to travel today?'

'As far as time permits. We're over-near the coast as yet, I shall feel happier as we distance ourselves from the Channel.'

Georgina nodded. 'Where precisely are we? I expected to see the busy streets of the port when I looked out this morning.'

'We are on one of the coaching runs, a few miles inland.'

'And where are we heading?'

'Eventually to Paris. I hope one day to provide a book about that city. Normally, I take a short preliminary visit to assess the time I will require for the task.'

Again, Georgina nodded.

'You need not concern yourself with this portion of our tour, I can think of no useful purpose you will serve there.'

'Very well.' Bewildered by his brusqueness, she gazed down at her plate. Howard had seemed, she'd thought on seeing him again, to be as pleased as she was, by the prospect of the weeks ahead. Evidently she had mistaken courtesy for interest in herself. She must beware that his good manners did not mislead her in the future. She'd been idiot enough already to think one night spent in his arms had revealed his feeling for her. She would not add to her folly by even attempting to fathom what he intended regarding their marriage. She was here to work, and in so doing to prove herself the equal of her predecessor. She would show that she would be as professional as any man.

Returning to their room to prepare for leaving, Howard saw his ring, discarded on the floor. His back to Georgina, he sighed as he placed it in his pocket.

Throughout their slow journey towards Paris in the carriage that Howard had hired, Georgina remained perplexed by his attitude. And when he stated coldly that he saw no reason for them to continue sharing a room, she did not argue.

But how could she not care when Howard took a whole day to wander with her through some fine city, urging her to pause and draw its cathedral, gold-washed in a light that held more than promise of an early spring? Or when he strolled beside the moat of a crenellated château, a hand on her shoulder while he related its history? Or again, more dangerously perhaps, when together they witnessed the sun sinking over a pastoral valley and learned they shared a longing to faithfully reproduce its beauty?

'So often I feel no work of mine will ever be adequate . . .' She had paused. 'Perhaps the two crafts together . . .' she had ventured, then fallen silent, rebuking herself for inviting a rebuff.

Howard, however, had nodded.

'Complementing each other as they do.'

He had stiffened then, as if to suggest some barrier prevented their work continuing. Georgina, sensing his withdrawal, had decided too much between them was unsettled. And one matter only could she untangle alone.

She wrote that night to Roland, telling him she could never become his wife. The facts looked bald on paper, yet she'd no wish to elaborate, explaining her marriage. She concluded the difficult letter by mentioning that they were travelling slowly across France, and were about to visit Paris.

One night short of the city they found great difficulty in obtaining accommodation. A fair had crowded every wayside inn.

They found at last one householder who seemed eager to offer hospitality.

The house was old and once had been the local manor. Its present owner, one Jean Doubrai, told them that he lived there with his sister, Marie.

Doubrai was an energetic man of some thirty years, robust, with black glossy curls combed towards pleasant features and eyes dark as Georgina's.

His sister was an older, paler edition, stiffening out now into fatness, but welcoming, and eager to please her unexpected guests.

Over dinner that night she equalled her brother in gregariousness but, to Georgina's regret, Marie had no English. Jean Doubrai, however, was anxious to air the language acquired during business visits to London for the wool trade.

He exercised his English on Georgina while Howard occupied Marie in her own tongue. And Georgina, admiring his proficiency in the language, gazed in Howard's direction, and felt the familiar longing that, despite all resolve, was aroused by his handsome appearance.

Tired with travelling, she and Howard were shown to their rooms immediately afterwards, and when he reminded her of the need for an early start next morning she wondered how she would rouse herself in time.

The bed was comfortable and Georgina slept soundly, for several hours, but then she awakened and, thinking back over the conversation of the previous evening, began wishing that *she* not Marie Doubrai, had held Howard's attention. She told herself that she was being foolish but the emotion remained, nevertheless, disturbing her until her mind became altogether too active for sleep.

She wondered what the time was and remembered that she had left her watch, together with tinder and flint, on the chest of drawers over by the window. She felt for her robe and slipped it on then walked barefooted across the carpet.

Cautiously, she ran a hand over the polished wood, trying to locate the candle. But somehow she knocked its silver holder, which fell to the floor with a dreadful clatter. She was kneeling, trying to find the candle, when a perfunctory rapping made her start.

She thought Howard was sleeping in the next door room. Had she so disturbed him that he came to rebuke her? She would cause no further irritation by keeping him out on the landing.

'Come in,' she called softly.

The man who entered was Jean Doubrai. Smiling, he glanced towards her. 'Is something amiss?'

'I am so sorry. I was careless. I wakened and came over here to light the candle . . .'

'. . . which is here.' Retrieving the silver candlestick, he placed it upon the chest and with a warm hand helped her to stand.

'I hope the candle-holder is not damaged.'

'I think not.' Doubrai, still smiling, scarcely glanced at it.

'You seem perturbed, is something wrong?'

She smiled. 'I could not sleep, wondered what the time was, and . . .'

'The night hours always seem the more solitary when one is wakeful. It is sad that you should be alone. Saunders keeps to his own room then?'

'Of course,' Georgina responded sharply.

'So, your collaboration does not extend beyond your work. But you cannot pretend that you enjoy lying there, with nothing but your thoughts.'

'I am quite . . .'

'. . . distressed? This way,' he insisted, taking her firmly by the arm and leading her from the room and along to a door standing ajar at the end of the landing.

Any disquiet evaporated when Georgina saw that the room was some kind of study, its walls book-lined, a great desk sentinel near the window. Doubrai closed the door softly behind them.

'This never fails,' he told her. 'I guarantee you will soon forget all matters that have troubled you.'

'Do you speak of some kind of potion?' Georgina began and was interrupted by his laugh.

Doubrai's dark eyes sought her gaze and

then he turned and, taking her hand, walked swiftly with her towards a large door which she supposed concealed a cupboard.

When he opened the door she saw that it gave on to a room that was quite dark and grew uneasy. But he propelled her through the door. His candle revealed that they stood in his bedroom.

'No,' she protested, but Doubrai was leaning towards her, his gaze holding hers before his lips covered her mouth.

Georgina struggled to push him away, but his solid frame anchored her against the wall.

'Now come, mademoiselle, you paid enough attention to me over dinner, do not pretend that I do not interest you . . .'

'That you can talk for a time on matters that do not bore me can give you no reason to assume . . .'

'That you'd welcome my embrace? I read desire in your eyes at table, I'm not unfamiliar with a woman who is aroused.'

'Then I wish you'd take yourself off to those who've acquainted you.'

'Clever!' He laughed. 'I have been busy. Is it not understandable that I now seek pleasant relief?'

'But not with a stranger.'

He pressed closer. 'That, *ma chère,* can be rectified. Indeed, I believed it had, for still I cannot accept that your glance this evening was indifferent. And where's the harm . . . ?'

'Harm? You would force yourself upon me, as though the matter were of no consequence?' Briefly, incredulity superseded her fear.

'Surely a woman who travels, as you do, with one who isn't her husband cannot expect belief in her innocence. Especially,' he thrust his head close to her own again, 'when her entire bearing is so provocative.'

His firm grasp prevented escape. As his arms closed about her, Georgina screamed. His lips silenced her cry and his probing tongue took advantage of her parted teeth.

Wrestling with him, Georgina was dismayed to learn how powerful he was. When he drew away his head for breath, she screamed again.

'He'll not hear you, no one will.'

'Howard, Howard!' she screamed while Doubrai spoke.

Again, a ferocious kiss silenced her. His hands were working over the back of her robe, slithering towards her thighs now as he thrust himself at her.

'Here's a man for you,' he declared crudely, 'don't tell me you feel nothing.'

His lips were at hers again, bruising them against her teeth.

'Get away if you can,' he challenged, 'if you still wish to! There's no reason to fear me, girl, I'm just as any other man — and better equipped than most, I'm told . . .'

The door beside them opened and Howard burst inside the room.

'Thank God,' Georgina breathed, leaning weakly against the wall.

'I was only . . .' Doubrai began. Howard appeared about to strike him. Doubrai shrugged and backed away.

Seizing Georgina's hand, Howard dragged her in silence along the corridor to her room. He pushed her inside and slammed its door, then went to light a candle and spoke with his back towards her.

'Dress yourself. We are leaving.'

'As soon as you go to your room,' she promised, still gasping breathlessly.

'*Now*, I say.' Slowly, he faced her. 'At this moment, madam, modesty ill becomes you.'

Her eyes gleamed with tears as she raised them to his chilling glance. 'Thank you, Howard, for rescuing me.'

'What else could I have done? It seems I was wrong to judge you were safe anywhere but in my sight!'

She forced herself to dress but removed her nightgown only after she had writhed into her chemise beneath it. Slipping on her gown, she struggled with trembling fingers to fasten the tiny buttons down its back.

'Here — let me, else we'll never quit this wretched house.'

His hands were icy at her neck, yet her skin tingled as though burned by his touch; she closed her eyes, longing to recognize forgiveness in more reassuring contact. But Howard walked stiffly away to the farthest corner of the room.

'And now attend to your packing.'

'But what of your own — or are you ready for leaving?'

'Do you think I'd dare leave you alone? Not under this roof — I doubt that I'll risk leaving you unchaperoned anywhere, even for one moment!'

Insulted by his implication that she couldn't be trusted in male company, she was infuriated, but swallowed her anger.

In Howard's room she was made to sit while he went into the adjoining dressing-room then rapidly packed his belongings.

By the time they were riding into Paris that afternoon Georgina felt completely dejected.

The inn where they found accommodation was superior to any that she had visited before, however, and after changing her gown her spirits began rising. It was cautiously, nevertheless, that she joined

Howard for the evening meal. She was afraid the events of the past twelve hours had so taxed his patience that he'd not think twice about sending her back to England.

Howard, meanwhile, had been thinking. Was it not Georgina's very innocence — an attribute that he loved — which had made her unable to recognize danger.

'Tomorrow,' he began, during dinner, 'we will visit the Consular Palace of the Tuileries, and the Louvre — I suppose you'll complain if I neglect that wealth of sculpture and paintings.'

Georgina ventured a smile. 'You think then that you might tolerate my company?'

Howard snorted but then he laughed, astonishing her. 'The incident in the night proved the truth of my warning.' He handed her the brass ring. 'Whether you care to or not, you'd best wear this — I've arranged that you'll sleep in my room.'

Relieved, Georgina resolved never again to give him anxiety. But though they shared a bed he paid her no more heed than if she'd been a waxen dummy.

'You were born to your work, weren't you?' Georgina commented while they strolled beside the Seine next day. 'You have to convey your own enthusiasm to everyone else.'

Howard smiled, for once appearing pleased.

'I suppose I do attempt something like that,' he admitted. 'Although I was unaware of it today. Life isn't only work.'

As soon as the words were out he wished them back. While she remained besotted with Crowbrook *he'd* not give her the satisfaction of learning how her company delighted him.

They were feeling elated though as they returned to the inn that evening. Georgina had been overjoyed by Howard's including her in this tour of the city, whilst he could not deny being happier for her presence.

As they entered, the innkeeper's wife drew them aside. Smiling, she enquired about their outing.

'Wonderful!' Georgina exclaimed. 'We have seen so much.'

'Then you will not regret missing the friend who called, asking for the two of you . . .'

Already, Howard had paled. 'Are you sure it was us that he sought? I cannot imagine that any man would know our whereabouts.'

'This gentleman knew of your visit to Paris, and was touring all the inns, seeking you.'

'And the fellow's name?' Howard demanded.

'I must apologize, monsieur, I cannot recall his name. The mail coach came into the yard causing such confusion that . . .'

'All right, no more,' Howard snapped, taking Georgina's arm as he led her to a small unoccupied room. 'This cannot be!' he exclaimed. 'How can they have traced me here? I have told no one of our itinerary, have even changed our route to take in Paris. Anyone seeking me would imagine us halfway to Florence.'

'Perhaps some friend, learning that you are in Paris, wishes to renew acquaintance?'

'I have no friends,' he stated icily, releasing her arm.

'Oh come — what of the Mallaigs, — and your acquaintance in York?'

'What do you know of him?' Howard asked sharply.

'Only that — that you visited . . .'

'Don't you dare speak of him again! Who have you told about him?'

'No one. Why should I?'

'Because you delight in concerning yourself in my affairs.'

'That's not true!'

'It must be. *I* have told no one we were coming here.'

'Howard,' she said gently, laying a hand on his arm, 'surely you've no reason to be afraid.'

'You learned from your father that I was compelled to quit Portugal.'

'And you never explained the reason.'

'Why should I?'

Georgina breathed deeply before responding slowly: 'Perhaps because I'm sufficiently concerned to want to understand.'

'Understand! Ha! There's one thing alone that you should understand — that I keep my own counsel and hope that others might respect matters that are my business alone. I'll give account of my affairs to no man, nor to woman either!'

'I am not asking that you should, but I am anxious when you become so perturbed each time anyone enquires for you.'

'Would you enjoy your life being endangered?'

'No, but . . . why are you so certain yours is?'

His manner changed, despondency replacing anger. 'Treason has but one penalty, hanging.'

Life had grown all the dearer these past weeks; a feeling increased now by the transparent regard in those brown eyes.

Georgina lowered her gaze. 'But you wouldn't commit treason, would you?'

'If you have to ask that then you have not known me.' He turned from her.

'Howard.' Georgina was reaching for his arm again when a loud knock startled them both. Together, they faced the door.

'The gentleman is returned, monsieur, may I show him in?'

Glancing to Howard, Georgina saw that his complexion resembled marble. His body took on the rigidity of that same substance.

Curtly, he nodded. *'S'il vous plaît...'*

CHAPTER EIGHT

'Georgina!'

Striding into the room, Roland took both her hands.

Half-laughing in relief, she glanced at Howard. 'See, it is Roland! There was no necessity for our . . .'

Evidently unconsoled by similar feelings, Howard appeared only slightly less agitated than before. He stalked from the room.

'What ails him?' Roland enquired as he went to close the door.

Georgina shook her head. 'I do not know,' she lied, and sensed how committed she was to supporting Howard.

As Roland tried to embrace her, she drew away. But, reluctant to have her family learn through him of her marriage, she told him simply that she had meant every word of her letter and their betrothal was ended. He pleaded that she reconsider; he had come to Paris with plans to take her home, but Georgina remained adamant and he went striding out of the inn.

Unable to gain admittance to the room

she shared with Howard, she sent a message, asking if he were dining with her.

The sudden knocking at the door startled Howard. His gaze flew to the window, seeking escape. Again, the rapping sounded. He left the bed and walked cautiously to the door. Opening it, he remained half-concealed behind its panels, ready to retreat.

One of the inn's porters smiled and touched his brow. 'Mr Saunders, sir, I have a message from the lady, who asks if you are dining . . . ?'

'Thank you, no. I have no appetite.'

Shutting the door, Howard leaned heavily against it. Lord, how scared he'd been. Even despite his recent resolve that once Georgina left for England he would follow.

At Dover he would surrender to the authorities and, even if wrongly judged, would accept the punishment. That way he'd be free, in time. Or dead. And freed from fear.

Going slowly over to the bed, he sank once more upon it. And sank also into the despondency brought by Crowbrook's arrival. How could Georgina expect that he would eat with them, making conversation, when all the while he knew that they sought only to be rid of him and in each other's arms? How, when he ached to hold her

149

close, could he watch the man devouring her with small grey eyes? How keep his mind from the evidence around her throat of the desire consuming the pair?

Howard flung across the bed, biting into the pillow, hating his need of her and the way it had changed life. He had loved the game he'd played, outwitting those who plotted his capture — until responsibility for this beloved girl had sobered him.

It had taken Georgina to teach him that grown men should not toy with the authorities. That not only must he be honourable in the tasks he undertook, but must also be *seen* to be so. And not risk accusations.

Accusations . . . He had almost believed she trusted him. But then her expression of doubt had crushed such illusions. And that had hurt. There'd been much to crush him recently. Friends, like the Laird, had turned him from their homes. Others, not risking friendship with a spy, had dropped his acquaintance. He bore them no grudge; and bore Georgina none.

If only he could feel nothing. And there was some hope. God alone knew how feeling gnawed at his strength. And most of all this ever-present ache to belong to her body.

Howard groaned. Was this, maybe, the reason for his failure? That desire that haunted his nights, and enhanced the days they'd spent together. Had it been so wrong to want her?

Again, someone rapped, again he started. This time he made no move to answer. Already, he'd decided to let them take him for trial. *Without her,* what did anything matter?

The door creaked as it opened. Howard remained motionless, face pressed into the pillow.

'Are you ill?'

The voice was hers. Why was she not hastening with Crowbrook to England? Or bedding with him beneath this roof?

'Howard what is it? Are you indisposed?'

Her skirt brushed his tightly-breeched leg. Leaning over, she gently turned him to face her.

'You are ill . . .' Cool fingers eased his forehead. He longed to hold her against him.

Not looking at her, he spoke. 'I believed you were gone.'

She laughed, but gently. 'Did you now? And thought to be rid of the responsibility that I bring?'

'No, I . . . No.'

'What then? Were you glad to be alone at last, to be free of this female who must needs have you dashing to her rescue?'

'No.'

'I judged it my turn to . . . to investigate your absence. I feared something might have happened . . .'

'And now you know that it has not, you may leave with Crowbrook.'

'Roland has left.'

'Alone?'

'Well, I am here. Unless he's found another, I imagine he is unaccompanied.'

'But . . .' Incredulously, with hope warming him, Howard stared at her.

Still smiling slightly, Georgina crossed to look out of the window, her back to him. 'I found I couldn't feel certain that I would have no regrets if I went with Roland.'

'Oh?'

Howard left the bed. Coming to her, he took her shoulders, turning her so that he might see her face.

'I have embarked on a career,' she said evenly. 'I would not abandon it.'

'Is it career alone that you would not abandon?' He wished the question unspoken as he dreaded her reply.

Georgina said nothing. Only the steady regard of her eyes gave him answer — and one that sent his pulses racing.

She swallowed. 'We'll not enjoy the visit to Tuscany as we should, though, while you're so wary. Don't you think it time you

152

confided your fears?'

'And have you run away from me?'

'If running were my wont, I'd be heading towards England, now.'

'Very well. But my mission in Portugal was for an acquaintance and cannot be divulged.'

'Oh.'

'But I may reveal a fraction of the matter. Did your father tell you I am suspected of spying for the French?'

'He mentioned something of that nature.'

'How calm you are. Don't you realize what such a charge can mean?'

'Oh, yes.' Her splendid eyes darkened with a gloss of tears. 'But surely,' she continued slowly, 'we'll only survive by refusing to panic.'

He nodded. 'So I have believed. And now I'll fight to remain so elusive that none will catch me.'

'Howard! That is no way to live — can't you tell them the truth?'

'*Were the secret mine*, yes. But success depends upon absolute discretion. There is no means of ensuring that whilst proving my innocence.'

'I wish I understood.'

'The Portuguese discovered maps that I had made.'

'Maps? But they could have been for your books.'

'They were not, and those who expelled me had learned they were not.'

'But why were they so incriminating?'

'They detailed routes to the ports.'

'I see. But couldn't this friend speak up for you?'

'How could he? He needs secrecy.'

'You'd risk all this for friendship?'

He snorted. 'Not for friendship alone, he'll pay well for all information.'

'Oh.'

'I'm not a wealthy man, Georgina.'

'But . . .' He'd puzzled her again. She remembered the house where they'd first met, glanced to his elegant clothing.

'The house, as I told you, is my cousin's. I also . . .' he paused, reluctant to continue, '. . . owe money which paid my early travels to write the first book.'

'I thought that volume, and your others, have done well . . .'

'And so they have, but my profession isn't lucrative, especially when it involves thousands of miles of travel.'

Going down late to dine they found a large company assembled, fiddlers playing and people dancing. As they ate they watched, and when they left their table Howard surprised her by taking her arm and leading her towards the dancers.

A young man lavishly dressed in blue silken coat, white breeches and a richly embroidered shirt, was demonstrating some new step with a girl who wore a pink gown that floated around her as she moved.

'This is the waltz,' Howard whispered, 'introduced by Napoleon's troops.'

And then the young couple were inviting everyone to try the new dance. Howard's hand went to Georgina's waist and, laughing, he insisted that they join in. She stumbled as she attempted the steps, but Howard seemed to know the waltz and, surrendering to its rhythm, she began to relax.

Despite this glimpse of a new aspect of her husband, Georgina was not sorry when he told her that they would leave for Florence in the morning.

Travelling for eight or nine hours in a day, they eventually reached the Danube. All along their route they had been kept aware by troops and supplies on the move, of the war in Europe. Here, where the river was navigable to flat-bottomed boats, they were utilized for men as well as ammunition and provisions. Georgina, wondering how they had escaped all fighting, imagined Howard sufficiently foresighted to plan to avoid Bonaparte's campaigns.

Hearing distant gunfire filled her with dismay, but she determined to conceal her fears. She had to prove herself staunch as any man.

The postillion hired with their carriage halted and came to speak urgently with Howard.

'There's cavalry, following the line of the river, hundreds of them. We'd best not continue that way tonight, sir.'

'Won't they have passed ahead of us?' Howard enquired. The Danube here was some distance from the road, just visible from the hill where they had stopped.

The man shook his head. 'They're making camp, I reckon preparing for a dawn attack on some town.'

Howard left the carriage and went with him to inspect the situation. Returning to her, he appeared exhilarated by the hazard.

'We'll return to the town Georgina, and put up for the night. There's nothing to fear, but we can go no further until Bonaparte's men move on.'

The post-chaise was turned about but as they approached the town they saw hordes of blue-uniformed infantrymen thronging the streets and spilling from the ancient walls. The French army had evidently occupied the town almost as soon as they had left.

'Confound it!' Howard exclaimed. 'We'll find no rest here this night.' He banged on the carriage side, alerting the postillion.

'You know the area, man, what do you advise?'

'There's one chance, sir. I have a sister whose husband farms a few acres south of here. If we reach her she'd give you a bed.'

'Do not hesitate then.'

Smiling, Howard turned to Georgina. 'You see? Already we have a solution.'

The carriage rattled and shook over the road, rutted by the passing army.

'I'll tell them where we're bound,' the postillion called as they neared the first of Napoleon's men. As he did so, Georgina sensed immediately that something was amiss.

The officer's tone was brusque and he shook his head, pointing vehemently down the road.

Their postillion shouted, and waved his arms at the officer who flicked a commanding wrist to bring soldiers running to support him.

'*Allez-vite!*' the officer cried. But the postillion stolidly held their carriage still.

'He's telling them he has a sister in the vicinity, they'll let us through now,' Howard reassured Georgina.

She heard a shot, and then another.

'Oh, God!' Howard exclaimed. She turned towards him.

The horses reared and Georgina shut her eyes, terrified.

'Oh, no!' Howard gasped.

She opened her eyes just as their postillion slithered to the ground. Already, blood stained his coat.

'He's not dead?'

'Looks like . . .' Howard began, about to leave the post-chaise. But the horses, frenzied, lurched this way then the other, dragging the carriage with them.

The officer roared an order and one of his men seized the reins of one horse and struck it on its side. The animal screamed, a terrible, distraught sound. Suddenly the post-chaise swung off the road and they hurtled over the undulating field.

Georgina clung to Howard, petrified, her teeth juddering. A shot was fired but seemed to strike only a glancing blow. And then all was quiet behind them.

Howard looked searchingly all around, then hugged her. 'They're not pursuing. We're safe now, Georgina.'

'You can't know that. They might send cavalrymen after us.'

'I doubt there are any garrisoned in the town. And they've no cause to, we're no threat to them.'

'Then why did they shoot our postillion?'

Howard frowned. 'There, you have me — a whim perhaps, or maybe he provoked the officer.'

'But what can we do?' She glanced wildly about, as trees flashed by them and hooves thundered over the turf. 'We'll both be killed!'

'Presently, they will steady. Then I'll take the reins. Do not fret, my love, we'll soon gain the road again.'

'But — but can you drive a post-chaise?'

Howard laughed. 'I'm damned if I'll be beaten by a carriage!'

And soon the horses, tiring, slowed near a group of trees.

Howard touched her arm. 'Hold on to the seat if things become rough, but I'll try to maintain an easy pace once I have the horses in hand.'

She watched uneasily while he went to calm them. Whatever would she do if Howard failed; she'd never control even one horse if he were somehow injured.

But soon he was driving steadily along the road that led away from the town. They passed the spot where they'd first sighted the army and Georgina noted thankfully that no troops appeared ahead.

Howard readily managed the horses and she leaned into her upholstered corner, breathing more evenly.

'Are you all right?' he called.

'Yes. Yes, thank you.'

'The soldiers must have gone on ahead.'

They had travelled under a mile when he slowed the carriage abruptly where one of the few hills in the area provided a vantage point. She saw his shoulders slump, and joined him, looking to see what had caused his dejection.

Below them lay the Danube, spanned by a bridge which was scarcely visible beneath horse-drawn gun carriages. The setting sun glinted off red-plumed helmets then vanished, turning infantry and cavalry from individuals into a menacing blur that stretched over both river banks into concealing woods. The sight had a kind of fearful splendour.

'What will we do?' she asked.

'What can we do, but stay here the night.'

'But . . .'

'The carriage is comfortable, we'll be in the dry if it should rain, and sheltered from any wind.'

'We can't . . .'

'We cannot cross the Danube by that bridge, and that is certain.'

'No, but there must be another bridge.

160

And the troops are nowhere near this road.'

'So far as we're aware. There'll be guards, though, posted to alert their camp to any who approach. We'd best remain where we are.'

'I do not wish to.'

'I do not trust the French when roused. Remember how they behaved towards our postillion, who had no quarrel with them.'

'But . . .'

'Tell me a better scheme.'

Georgina grew silent, pondering. There must be some means of avoiding a night out here.

'Is there no other town where we might go?'

'Our horses are exhausted, they'll drop in the road if we force them much further. I'll not risk them to preclude our slight discomfort.'

Howard glared out across the valley.

'I know I'm the last person you want near you. Twice, I've saved you from those who'd sample your delights. Do you class me with such brutes?'

'Of course not, I . . . Howard!'

He'd turned abruptly from her and was striding away. 'I'm to the carriage,' he snarled over his shoulder. 'You must do as you think most seemly!'

CHAPTER NINE

The distance to the post-chaise felt like miles as Georgina walked reluctantly towards it. She was wondering how on earth they would pass the night in anything resembling civility.

'It is somewhat chilly now,' she said, after taking a breath to ward off any tremor in her voice as she opened the door.

'Indeed.'

The interior of the carriage, darkening now, gave her no hint of Howard's expression.

'I think perhaps you are wiser to be settling in here,' she prattled, reminding herself of her mama's inconsequential chatter.

'Oh, yes?' His tone sounded cold. He made no move to assist her up the step.

'And I see that you have sensibly drawn the post-chaise into the lee of those rocks.'

'I'm delighted to learn of your approval.' His voice was flat, totally enigmatic.

'Am — am I still welcome to share . . . ?'

The gloaming revealed a movement of his shoulders. Was he so indifferent to her company? About to step into the carriage, she hesitated, one foot hovering.

His chuckle startled her, sounding loud on the night air.

'Oh, Georgina, come . . .'

Both hands seized her own as, still laughing, he helped her up to sit beside him. Closing the door, he shook his head. And then he laughed again.

'Your evident relief is ruining all pretence of appearing independent!'

'And does that matter when, from the start, you've enjoyed taking charge, of our situation — and of me!'

'I doubt anyone's capacity for the latter.'

'You've got a clever tongue, Howard Saunders. Is that because words are your trade?'

'If you say so.'

'Don't pretend compliance. I've known you some while now . . .'

'*And* intimately . . .'

Her gaze, accustoming to the gloom, linked with his and read there a brilliant appraisal, amused and provocative. She loved him like this, why was he so often sombre?

'You could permit yourself use of my shoulder — for comfort. And, if it'll not frighten you too greatly, an arm about you will ward off any chill.'

'You are most kind.' The mocking bite in

her tone belied the warmth growing within her.

His shoulder was indeed comfortable, and as he stirred to encircle her with an arm she caught the scent of the soap he'd used earlier. There was an open-air freshness also, reminding her of linen dried in the garden. She found another smell too, of new cloth, and felt his shirt crisp against her cheek.

'Your shirt is new.'

'Lord,' he exclaimed, 'the girl must have spared me a glance at last! I'd have sworn you took no account of what I might be wearing.'

'You dress well, and I have noticed,' she asserted before laughter revealed his teasing.

'There's been little time for . . . noticing anything.'

Georgina was quiet. Even the horror of seeing a man shot had waned now, to have not more effect than some half-remembered nightmare.

'If you rise with the dawn,' he told her, 'you might draw the military scene down yonder.'

'You know I specialize in topography.'

'And long words! Oh, you'd be no Turner or Schwebach, agreed — but you can produce a presentable copy.'

'Thank you.'

'And you never know where your talents lie till you try something fresh . . .'

Turning towards her, he was searching her eyes. His own had deepened to cobalt. Some force was pulling her to him, closer than any contact of limb against limb, closer even than the breath caressing her cheek. And with this man she would explore everything.

Once only had she felt this attuned with him, and then her entire being had begged her for a union which had proved more wonderful than she had dared dream. Here, though, there could be no such fulfilment — even if he'd reciprocated her own yearning.

Relaxing a little, she nestled into his side.

The silence that developed was easy. His heart was a reassuring beat, scarcely perceptible, yet ceaseless as the tracking of moon across the sky out there. Hearing and feeling its rhythm, Georgina drifted in and out of consciousness.

For a time she fought sleep, savouring the sensation of being held, of feeling secure. And *wanted*. Were not supposing herself wanted here a presumption — a dream of what might have been. If they were thus alone, in reality, if Howard had no Lady Virginia awaiting him in London.

Wearied, Georgina slept. Howard knew no such release. As long as the final glimmer of daylight lasted, his eyes turned towards the French camp, while ears strained for any threat. And when darkness enveloped their post-chaise, and silence from the army assured him they were resting, he still forced himself to stay alert.

He was neither worried nor unhappy now. All the fears of being captured, tried, and imprisoned were, for the time, suspended. All thought of the debt he owed and necessity for its repayment ceased to plague him, and he luxuriated in the present.

His wife whom, but a few hours ago, he'd imagined taken from him was nearer now than he had hoped she might ever be. His arms were her protection.

Her hair against his chin was silk-textured, warm, scented. He moved his free hand to press her head against him.

Georgina eased herself closer, murmuring sleepily as if in approval. He smiled to himself. A deep tenderness caught at his throat, as the evenness of her breathing seemed to him like the pulsating of a gentle clock.

Her breast was at his ribs, pressing its pert cone at him, as if to assert her sensuality. A reminder he'd no need of and without which he'd have been more comfortable. Yet it was a part of her; just as making love had been a part of knowing her. For she was complete woman, his whole being approved her as such.

He longed to plant kisses first on her hair, then brow, cheek . . . until the sweetness of her lips was his. Kisses to rouse her — from sleep and into awareness — so that the throbbing of her slender body might assure him of an interest grown mutual . . .

But this was neither time nor place for such thoughts. He had waited, and he would wait, for renewal of the giving and taking that was ultimate commitment. He must be content now with the feel of head against his shoulder, hair beneath his lips, thigh touching thigh . . .

As recognition of each separate delight triggered sense into life, desire grew. A tingling, along arm and about ribs, through each part of him in contact with her. And, within him, a surging force against which he clenched fists and stiffened, willing its power into acquiescence.

Disturbed, Georgina moved. He held his breath, fearing he had wakened her.

Once more she settled, quietly, into the circle of his arm. Howard gnawed on his lip, wrestling with the ache to end all pretence of accepting her indifference, in a glorious storm of passion. And then he remembered how reluctant she'd been to even spend the night out here with him. He'd beg favours of no woman; he'd live with the longing she created.

He groaned.

'Howard?' Instantly awake, she tried to discern his expression in the darkness. 'What is it?'

'Nothing,' he murmured.

She leaned again into his shoulder.

His kiss was light and, contrary to instinct, on her forehead.

Sounds of activity from the French camp awakened them at dawn. Howard and Georgina marvelled at the efficiency of Napoleon's forces as they prepared to move onwards. The army thundered away from the bridge and presently they were able to take their carriage across.

'There'll be no more diversions now,' Howard told her. 'I'd hoped to take you to Vienna, but I'll not risk further encounter with the French.'

They stopped at the next posting inn for a replacement postillion, and fresh horses. Georgina was feeling none the worse for her strange night and also greatly relieved to have heard Howard's declaration that he mistrusted the French. Surely this proved the charge of spying had no foundation.

After breakfasting they headed south into the Alps.

'Although there'll be no more detours,' Howard said, 'I have arranged that we stay two nights in Innsbruck with friends. I shall show you some of the splendours of that city.'

Because of his promise, Georgina looked forward to reaching this destination. And even the pleasant scenery along their route was no longer compensating for soreness induced by too much travelling. But they saw no hint on this road of Bonaparte's army.

'We should have left them far behind now we've quit the Danube,' Howard said. 'They are fully engaged with the Austrians.'

The afternoon was brilliant with sunlight when Georgina saw Innsbruck spread before them in its lush valley.

Sensing Howard watching her, she turned to smile.

'How exquisite!'

He smiled back and nodded to himself, as though he had anticipated her appreciation aright.

Soon they were climbing again to the south, until they reached a large Austrian chalet which had an overhanging roof to protect it from avalanches. Howard called the postillion to stop.

He led Georgina swiftly towards the middle-aged lady who had come out to stand on the steps, her smile broad as her ample figure.

'Frau Fussen!' Howard greeted her, with a warmth that took Georgina by surprise.

'Frau Fussen, this is Miss Morton, who is an artist — what do you think to that? She is a gifted illustrator.'

Frau Fussen's English was limited to an exchange of courtesies, yet Howard's expression as the woman spoke in rapid German conveyed his delight.

He placed a hand on Georgina's shoulder as they followed their hostess into a wood-panelled entrance hall.

'Frau Fussen is amazed that one so young is capable of working to my high expectations! I am pleased she approves you, she is dear to me — and, indeed, replaces the family which I lack.'

Frowning slightly, Georgina gazed at him. She slipped a hand into his.

Frau Fussen turned at the foot of the stairs after instructing servants who came to carry their baggage.

'I have such a surprise for you, Howard. One that will keep no longer. Your cousin is visiting with us . . .'

'The — the Lady Virginia?'

'*Ja*,' Frau Fussen replied, and added some phrase that Georgina didn't understand.

'I see.' Neither tone nor expression revealed Howard's emotion.

Georgina felt cheated and, now that her hand was released, discarded. She could scarcely believe the misfortune that had brought Virginia Mayburn to spoil her visit to Innsbruck.

At dinner that evening the three were reunited and, despite the presence of Frau Fussen and her husband Armand, Georgina felt so upset that even civility was difficulty.

Earlier, unpacking her belongings in her room, she had struggled to control the frustration that made her want to scream. She had fondly believed that here Howard would want to make her his again, for surely she'd seen desire in his gaze that night in the carriage. But on the way upstairs he had noticed the brass ring on her finger and had told her curtly that she'd be safe without it in the home of friends.

Sitting across the table from Lady Virginia, she wished she'd succumbed to the temptation to wear the ring and force him to acknowledge that they were married.

'I expected your arrival here some while ago,' Virginia said, her huge eyes, bright as the emerald gown she wore, at once reproachful and coquettish.

'Is that so?' his bland smile was enigmatic. 'Didn't I tell you we were visiting Paris on our way?'

Georgina wondered if he had withheld the information from Virginia, but feared she was reading her hope into his words. And now his cousin was glancing across the table towards her, the gaze of those green eyes sharply assessing.

'And were you impressed by the great city, Miss Morton?' she enquired. 'You must have found it very different from your country home.'

The question was asked patronizingly and Georgina glared back at the woman who had robbed her of all pleasure in the visit. 'I find large cities stimulating, and appreciate the skill with which their buildings are designed,' she said. And longed to add that living in the country did not necessitate that one became countrified.

She thought she detected the glimmer of a smile around Howard's lips as he paused while eating the excellent veal provided by their hostess.

'Miss Morton is looking forward to exploring Innsbruck with me,' he told his cousin, 'we are remaining here two nights for that purpose.'

'Two only?' Virginia demanded. 'But I thought . . . My dear, now that I am here I feel certain you will extend your stay.'

'I am sorry, no. I have work awaiting me in Florence and must not delay.'

'You imply that I would waste your time for you, Howard, you know that is not the case. I would remind you that I am the one who bears your rebuke for being often too serious.'

The snarl in her voice drew Howard's stare. 'I suggest, dear cousin, that you refrain from boring others with rehearsal of our private disagreements.'

Lady Virginia's pale countenance threatened to equal the flare of her elaborately-styled locks. For a second, she lowered her gaze to her plate, but she recovered swiftly to deliver another barb in Georgina's direction.

'So, you work for your living? Has no one offered for your hand?'

Georgina didn't know how to respond. Howard saved her the problem of replying.

'Miss Morton is pursuing her profession whilst travelling and seeing other countries. As to marriage, even your limited perception, Virginia, must grant that she will have no shortage of offers . . .'

For a moment Georgina felt the keenness

of his blue eyes, but was unable to meet their gaze while his cousin was alert for her response.

'You have indeed a beautiful companion,' Herr Fussen put in, smiling warmly towards Georgina. 'How fortunate that young ladies are now beginning to venture about the world.'

'*Some* always have done so,' Lady Virginia interjected. 'Whilst others consider it more maidenly to remain at home.'

'Since you have travelled all this way, unaccompanied,' Howard remarked smoothly, 'I wonder in which category you place yourself.'

Lady Virginia's swift intake of breath was her only response. And Howard, perhaps feeling remorse, asked Herr Fussen's advice in planning an itinerary that would ensure that none of Innsbruck's sights be missed.

He was obliged to include Lady Virginia, however, when she said she was interested in the outing. Georgina was so vexed that she asked to be excused the moment the meal was over.

The privacy of her room gave no consolation. She had just settled beneath the snowy counterpane when she heard Howard's voice and his cousin's on the terrace below her window. She forbade herself to listen, but Lady Virginia could not be ignored.

'You haven't said you're pleased to see me,' she reproved Howard, sounding coquettish again.

'I am surprised.'

'You must have known I would be lonely in London during your absence.'

'You have Mrs Veryan and the other . . .'

'*Servants!* Do you want me to gossip with them?'

'The entertaining you do when I am there suggests you never lack friends . . .'

'And well you know that I don't enjoy inviting anyone when you're not there to host for me, my dear.'

Howard's reply failed to reach Georgina and she was about to discipline her ears by covering them when Virginia's next remark jolted her.

'I have a mind to see something of Tuscany myself, you know I've never visited Florence. Since you'll be staying with Vicenzo and he is, after all, *my* acquaintance I shall accompany you.'

Howard's response was inaudible and Georgina gasped in utter dejection. That the woman could mar this stay in Innsbruck was bad enough, the prospect of having her with them in Florence was unbearable.

And now the cousins appeared to be murmuring together in intimate affection. Howard laughed and then Lady Virginia spoke again.

'You'll not repulse me now, I'll wager. You're too aware of the bond between us.'

Again, his answer couldn't be heard, but his cousin's was plain.

'I trust the artist child had not made you forget the claim I hold. Nor that I'm the one who initiated you in love's delights . . .'

'Virginia — I'll not make such matters public . . .'

Howard's protest was followed by the swift opening and swifter closing of the terrace doors as, Georgina supposed, they came into the chalet to find a place more suited to private embraces.

Recalling the night passed under Lady Virginia's roof in London, she believed that they would be going to the one room. He was *her* husband. How could she endure the thought of him making love to anyone else?

It was only her will that kept Georgina dry-eyed during that night. She would become the finest artist that Howard Saunders might wish — and that was one way that Virginia Mayburn could not gain his admiration!

Before going out next morning, Georgina decided to grant no one the satisfaction of seeing her distress.

'How brilliantly it gleams!' she exclaimed, when Howard showed her the magnificent Golden Roof. 'And you say it was made for Duke Friederich?'

He nodded, evidently pleased by her enthusiasm. And when he took them to the superb Triumphforte, the arch raised by the Empress Maria Theresa of Austria, she was so ecstatic that she wondered if perhaps she was overdoing her excitement.

Before leaving on the following day they saw the river Inn as it flowed through the city, and sampled some of the excellent *kuchen* on offer in the coffee houses. And it was as they were sitting indulging in the rich confections that Howard lost his temper with Lady Virginia. They had been talking about the journey through the Alps when she observed loudly: 'And you're taking the route over the Brenner Pass towards Bolzano and Florence . . .'

Howard had stiffened in his seat as she began speaking. He glared at her, the blue eyes dark as any soldier's uniform.

'I was not offering the information for common knowledge!' he snarled.

Georgina wondered at the woman's lack of caution. But surely he was being needlessly apprehensive. Gazing around, she saw only a usual mixture of nationalities, some people looking so familiar that she might have been sitting in just such a place in England.

Howard urged them to hasten, however, so that they could bid farewell to the Fussens. And then he was hustling Georgina from the chalet and to the post-chaise hired for the journey. Assisting her inside, he closed the door after them.

Bewildered, Georgina glanced towards the corner where Lady Virginia's musky perfume lingered from the morning's outing.

'Isn't — isn't your cousin accompanying us?'

CHAPTER TEN

'Do you feel the need of a chaperone?' Howard enquired, his expression inscrutable.

'Why no.' Georgina wondered how to explain without revealing her eavesdropping. 'I — I understood that your cousin wished to go to Florence.'

He laughed. 'Her wishes did not coincide with my own.'

Georgina's elation seemed matched by their eager pace as the horses drew their carriage through the outskirts of Innsbruck. As she glanced back over the city from the mountain road she sensed its magic again, and regretted having allowed herself to be deflated by Lady Virginia.

Howard appeared to be in excellent spirits; supposing this resulted from his reunion with the fiery cousin, she resolved never to forget that he had this consuming passion for the woman.

As they climbed into the mountains, he told her about Florence, flattering her by commenting on her artistic appreciation.

When they stopped for the night Georgina felt quite exhausted by the concentration demanded by her attempt to remain modestly level-headed.

The inn was small, and they its only guests that night, but even though Howard did not share her room she slept dreamlessly to awaken at dawn eagerly anticipating their journey.

The next stretch over the Brenner Pass was arduous, steep, with a roughly surfaced road little more than a track. Here and there it narrowed so that it seemed they could plummet over sharp rocks into the ravine. They saw jagged peaks, some of which were snow-covered.

Georgina marvelled at their majestic beauty, but was alarmed by the prospect of what would befall them if their post-chaise left the road. Clamping her lips together lest she betray her fear, she tried to arrange her features in a smile.

Howard was struggling to compose the excitement he felt each time they were alone. Since leaving the Fussens' home he had relished being able to devote his entire attention to his wife. If Virginia had but known, her presence in Innsbruck had made her blatant sensuality repugnant. How disgusted he had been when she had hung about him, angling for an invitation to his room.

He took Georgina's hand, his fingers caressing hers — in reassurance, he would have claimed, yet the soft skin beneath his touch induced a stronger feeling. Memory resurrected the joy of arousing her body with his own until they both had sought consummation. And he knew now that he'd have no peace until he ceased this monkish existence and claimed her again. Tonight perhaps, in some quiet chalet. He could not bear that they should waste this time when they should be happy in each other.

Towards evening one of their horses struck a boulder beside the narrow road. The carriage tilted precariously sideways.

Georgina stifled her scream but gazed, horrified, while the next horse toppled, hurling the postillion from its back. The carriage somehow righted itself but, yelling, the man went tumbling down the craggy hillside.

'Sit quite still,' Howard bade her. 'I must take a look . . .'

He sprang down and ran towards their postillion who was lying on a narrow strip of grass.

Georgina opened the window, to try and see what Howard had found.

'Is he badly hurt?' she called, but Howard seemed not to hear.

Suddenly a face was thrust around the post-chaise.

'So — we meet again,' an English voice exclaimed, but she failed to recognize the face so close to her own.

'You remember us, surely?' said a voice from her other side and Georgina found herself staring into the eyes of one of the men who'd questioned her when she and Howard were returning from Scotland.

'She remembers *you*, Jack,' his colleague laughed.

Georgina remembered also the harsh rebuke that she'd earned from Howard by speaking with them.

'What do you want?' she demanded, hoping she sounded stern.

'We seek that spying rogue.'

'Who *are* you?' she asked the large, thick-set man with shifty eyes.

'Loyal citizens of the country he's betrayed, that's who.'

'Aye, and with courage enough to take him back there, you as well if you cause us trouble,' the smaller man who looked like a weasel added.

'But . . .' Georgina began, but the other man interrupted. Both carried pistols.

'Look, miss, you'd best tend to your own skin. We're taking him, and any magistrate in England will be eager to charge him.'

From the corner of her eye Georgina saw that Howard had helped their postillion to his feet. She wondered anxiously if together they would be equal to fending off these men who had appeared from nowhere.

'Howard, take care . . .' she cried.

She got no further. A rough hand that smelled of horses slapped over her mouth.

'Now, lady, don't go warning him. He's only your employer, remember, save yourself. Your postillion seems none the worse for his fall, he'll drive you back over the pass.'

'Without Mr Saunders?' she said, freeing her lips of the hand. 'I'll not leave . . .'

The man shrugged. 'Then you're more fool than I reckoned you.'

Howard was attempting to hurry up the rocky mountainside, hauling the postillion with him.

'Leave her be,' he commanded. 'She's done no harm.'

'So you admit *your* guilt . . .'

'I'll admit nothing, but I'll wager it's my neck you seek and not the young lady's.'

'I'll grant you that.' The smaller man spat in the dust at Howard's feet. 'Spying scum, that's what you are — and deserving of no consideration.'

'Aye,' his companion endorsed, 'and many there are who're waiting to press charges . . .'

'Who on earth are you, that you attempt to seize me?'

'Jack Roberts.'

'Seth Taylor — and proud of the name now — it'll be remembered for your capture.'

'Listen — Roberts, Taylor, I've been misjudged, although I'm unable to prove that . . .'

'Pah!'

'Think we'd take your word!'

'Then spare the lady, let the carriage through and . . .'

'We'd a mind to do as you suggest.'

'Only now we think it best to keep the two of you together, like — so as not to have her telling tales. There might be those out here who don't understand our purpose.'

'There'll be a reward out for you in England.'

'And we mean to collect.'

'She'll take her chance along of us now,' Seth Taylor asserted.

'Aye,' his companion concurred, grinning and wiping slobby lips on his sleeve. 'And I reckon our journey'll be all the livelier for having her along.'

'You may imagine what you will,' Georgina stated coldly.

Howard faced her, and she watched both pistols adjust their cover of him. 'Georgina — please, get into the carriage and . . .'

Mid-sentence, he gazed in horrified disbelief towards the post-chaise as it rumbled speedily away from them. As the dust settled, Georgina saw all their belongings were stacked beside the road.

Turning to the men, Howard snapped, 'No doubt you have your own conveyance, concealed where you set that boulder in our path.'

'Clever!' Seth Taylor snorted. 'But it's a rougher ride than you imagine that awaits you!'

'Aye, we've no carriage. Horses we use — and a fine stallion we've brought for you. The lady will ride with one of us . . .'

Howard was about to protest but Jack Roberts jerked his gun. 'You'll not be forgetting we are armed, Saunders.'

They were led towards the horses which were hidden beyond a scree of rocks. They were not permitted to exchange even one word. Georgina looked on, her spirits sinking, while they forced Howard to mount the grey stallion then lashed him to its back. It was roped to a black horse which Roberts mounted swiftly, compelling her reluctant admiration.

'You'd best keep behind, Jack,' Seth Taylor said. 'I'll take the lady on in front — her life will guarantee his co-operation.'

Riding without saddle was uncomfortable enough, but anxiety caused Georgina to turn frequently, checking that Howard was following. Each time she swung round Taylor's pistol tapped the side of her head to force her to face the way they were going.

Darkness was falling swiftly now, the sun had long since dropped behind the Alps, tinging their peaks with pink. The beauty all about them seemed to sharpen Georgina's hopelessness.

'This'll do,' Taylor called over his shoulder as they reached a scattering of trees concealing a grassy dell.

'Then we'll make camp while sufficient light remains,' Roberts agreed.

They walked the horses down the gentle slope, then tethered them to trees.

Howard was left astride the horse, still lashed to its back, but Georgina was allowed to dismount.

Taking turns to guard their prisoners, the men lit a fire and cooked a rabbit they had snared. Despite her fear Georgina found she was famished and watched enviously as they devoured hunks from the carcass.

Suddenly she noticed Taylor had lain aside his knife while he used his teeth to clean a rabbit leg of meat. Casually, as though to warm herself at their fire, she strolled towards them. They continued eating, exchanging lewd comments about her, their mouths full, but paying her scant attention. As Taylor turned aside to fling the discarded bone into the trees, she bent swiftly and picked up the knife. Her heart pounded, but both men continued to chew impassively.

'I wonder if they'll save any food for us,' she said to Howard, forcing her walk to remain slow as she went towards him, the knife concealed in her sleeve.

Pretending to stroke the horse, she slit the rope in two places — where it tethered his wrists, and as it went around the animal's girth.

'Walk away now,' Howard whispered. 'We must wait for the right moment. Take your cue from me.'

When she reached the fire again, Howard called to their captors.

'Surely you can spare us something . . .'

Taylor laughed, shaking his head. 'Water is all you'll get — a man can last for days without food.'

'Water then,' Howard said swiftly. 'Give

us water, I'm parched.'

'Take your time,' Roberts told his companion. And Seth Taylor did indeed linger before sauntering towards him with a crude mug.

'Thank you,' Howard said tersely, but as he raised the mug a flick of his wrist sent the water into Taylor's eyes. And then Howard hurled himself on to his captor. Taylor crumpled and they rolled over and over together, fists flailing.

Taylor, more accustomed to a fight, had a clear advantage, and Roberts did not trouble to join in the affray but watched instead from over by the fire and shouted encouragement.

Horrified, Georgina saw Taylor thrust a knee into Howard's stomach and he fell back, winded. Suddenly she couldn't just stand there. She pounced on Taylor just as he was struggling to his feet. He went thudding to his knees beneath her, rage and shock mingling in his yell.

'That's enough,' Jack Roberts shouted and she sensed that he had his gun in his hand. She saw the butt of Taylor's pistol then, bulging his pocket, just within reach.

Praying she'd remembered all her father had taught her about handling firearms, she swung round and fired. She was amazed nevertheless when Roberts' pistol went crashing on to nearby rocks.

Wrestling again with Taylor, Howard had him by the throat, thumping his head on the ground.

'Get on to one of the horses,' he hissed to her, with a swift glance towards Roberts who was nursing a wounded arm.

Howard left Taylor moaning on the ground and hastily helped her to mount. He grinned as he took to the stallion's back and rode off beside her. 'You were right — you don't lack mettle!'

Even in the darkness, riding beside Howard seemed to be all that Georgina desired. When he told her that they must find shelter and rest, she demurred.

'Can't we continue in the saddle until daylight? That way we'd be well clear before those two come after us.'

'You're forgetting the horses! These two will have been ridden hard for days. We'll leave this track once I have my bearings. In all these rocks there will surely be at least one cave ...'

A suitable place was difficult to find, and it was some while later that Georgina, nearing exhaustion, was led up a steep incline to the cave Howard had discovered. He saw her settled into a corner with their possessions near to hand then turned back towards the entrance.

'Where are you going?' she demanded.

'Only as far as the road. The verge there was sandy. In case those two follow, I'll remove all trace of hoof-prints.'

'Please come back soon and safely.'

While Howard was away the minutes appeared suspended, and memory of their ordeal turned each chirping insect or scrape of a branch into a sound to alert thudding pulses and straining eyes.

Even Howard's returning footfalls sent a hand to her mouth, checking an involuntary cry.

'Howard?' she whispered as he entered the darkened cave.

She felt his lips against her hair. 'But for me, you'd be safe in your home. Which is where you'll rest again, just as swiftly as I am able to take you there.'

'No — no.'

'I'm returning you to Kent, and there's an end to it.'

Georgina felt torn — warmed by recognition of his concern for her, yet dreading their parting.

'But what of our work? Of the guide books you would write? What of the illustrations I'd do . . . ?'

Howard refused to discuss the matter. 'Try to sleep,' he advised, 'you are safe with me.'

Oh yes, she thought, and shivered. I am safe with you — so very safe — because you are totally committed to Virginia Mayburn. What a fool she had been to believe it was concern for her that had brought on his decision to send her home. She knew him well enough by now to know he'd not keep two women around him.

She remained wakeful but silent; hunched against him, for she was cold, but acutely aware of the arm he'd put around her, and of his steady breathing.

Her body was quiet for the present, but she had no doubt that she would experience again the excitement aroused by this man who was her husband. And she knew just as surely that her feelings towards him were more powerful through springing from love rather than desire alone.

Would it be better then that she go home? Would it be wiser to end this meaningless marriage that was no more to him than the cheap ring he'd given her? Could she endure another meeting with Lady Virginia, when too-fertile imagination tortured her with pictures brighter than any that she might paint — pictures of Howard embracing that woman?

Her brain went hurtling back and forth, testing one decision then another; first that she must leave, then that she would stay.

Disturbed, Howard leaned against the chill rock. His thankfulness at finding the cave had been short-lived. They had come through so much together since leaving Innsbruck; riding away from Roberts and Taylor, he'd felt closer than ever to Georgina. Yet he'd known even then that he must never again risk the horror of endangering her.

His arm tightened around her. This couldn't have been further removed from the life he'd have chosen for them. Georgina had brought him deep happiness, yet what could he give her?

She shifted restlessly and sighed.

'I told you to try and sleep,' he said.

'I can't.'

He spread his thick coat on the sandy ground and drew her down beside him. She was shivering, she would be shocked still by the fright they'd had. As he pulled her to him Georgina relaxed, curving against him.

'M'm, that's better,' she murmured.

Howard's pulse was racing, his body reminding him that she was his wife. She was pressing close as though to escape all harm. In a surge of protectiveness he sought her lips.

Her answering kiss called desire right

through him, his tongue probed while his fingers traced the curve of her breast.

Georgina felt him hard against her and thrilled to the hand that slid into her low neckline to fondle the smooth skin. His thighs were warming her own, she stirred as if coming to life and felt him moving against her.

'Oh, Howard.'

A tremor of delight coursed through her as he caressed her thighs. She leaned away slightly while he eased up her skirts, then the tingling spread through her as his touch aroused stronger urgency and excitement. Impatiently, Howard tore at his own buttons and crushed her to him.

Georgina gasped, exhilarated by his unmistakable eagerness, and pressed nearer to his firm strength. Her lips found his again, her tongue darted between his teeth. He was breathing swiftly, caressing her with his lean body.

He turned her on to her back as her thighs parted for him. The tremor she felt as he probed fiercely became a rhythmic vibration that drew him deep inside her. As they were joined, waves of delight pulsed in her, willing her to echo each thrusting until the great shudder of sheer joy flared like fire through them.

As Howard gradually stilled, Georgina luxuriated in the glorious peace of belonging to him. He kissed her gently; as she drifted into sleep she thought he murmured 'wonderful'.

He awakened to find the joy waning, displaced by awareness of having allowed passion to overrule all misgivings. Again, everything seemed spoiled. He'd taken her in a squalid cave when he should have provided the finest bridal bed.

When Georgina opened her eyes he was at the cave entrance, the crescent moon silvering his drooping shoulders. Bewildered, she wondered why he felt none of her elation. Had their coming together been no more than satisfaction of an intense hunger? And she seized as partner because no other was here?

The cry could have been her own perplexed protest, yet Howard also heard it and stood up swiftly.

'Ssh . . .' he cautioned softly, 'I'll swear that was Taylor's voice. Calling their horses, I shouldn't wonder — so they'll lead them to us.'

Even as he spoke one of the horses whinnied.

Georgina gasped, and felt Howard's hand tighten on her arm.

'We cannot remain here. Gather together what belongings you can carry and hand me the rest. If we leave now, we'll be further into the mountains by the time they find this cave.'

'Won't they follow us?'

'I'll chance that in preference to awaiting them here!'

'But — but we are armed now . . .'

'And so are they, remember. I'll not barter your life.'

Another shout, unmistakably Taylor's, interrupted him. Georgina hurriedly thrust some things she couldn't manage into Howard's arms.

'Good girl,' he approved.

Again, they heard Taylor, much nearer, and again his horse neighed to guide its master.

'Oh, God,' she cried, 'we're too late!'

CHAPTER ELEVEN

In the blackness beyond the cave Georgina stood motionless, trying to distinguish ground from sky.

Howard freed the horses so that they wouldn't betray the place where they'd rested.

'Take my hand. We've a hard climb ahead if the slope here is like the rest of this mountain.'

Not daring to voice her fears, Georgina thrust her hand into his, and felt his strong fingers secure her own.

She was breathless before they had cleared their own height above the cave, but drove herself on, refusing to be declared unfit to keep pace with him.

It seemed a long, wearisome climb before they risked a short respite, and they heard the voices of Taylor and Roberts, echoing from the craggy peaks until Georgina felt that the men's presence surrounded them.

'They're following us, I'm certain . . .' she whispered in alarm, but Howard squeezed her hand encouragingly.

'I think not, my sweet; they believe we're still on the road.'

'And when they don't find us there they'll come after us.'

'I doubt that, the wound you gave Roberts will need a surgeon's skill, they will head toward Bolzano.'

'They'll wait for us there! They will seize you and take you back to England, to be charged.'

'And do you suppose we would walk calmly into the town now — after our experience with them?' He shook his head. 'We'll make round it towards the south.'

'And aren't you afraid that they will trace us there?'

'We shall be staying with Conte Vicenzo. They will seek us only in coffee houses and inns.'

After they had paused to rest Georgina felt her strength returning, yet she was not convinced that they were not being pursued. She stared agitatedly about, trying to peer through the blackness, and starting at every wheeling bat or scurrying rodent.

They gained the summit as a pale line appeared between the mountain tops over to their left.

'Dawn is coming,' Howard murmured, placing an arm about her shoulders. 'And our spirits will rise. We have left those two behind, Georgina, there's nothing to fear.'

Only a little way down the mountainside a foot crunched on loose earth. Stones went scuttering down into the ravine. Georgina shuddered, her spine tingling, and pressed her face into Howard's shoulder. They heard more footfalls then, firmer, much closer to hand.

'Oh, Lord.' Howard seized her arm, urging her to run. 'Quickly, while darkness lasts.'

The surrounding blackness was all that concealed them, on this side of the peak the terrain was barren with neither rock nor tree large enough to offer cover.

'We do not stand a chance,' Georgina wailed, overcome by fear and tiredness.

'Think that, and we're finished,' Howard hissed. 'Would you stay here and have them take us?'

Miserably, Georgina shook her head, listening to the steady pounding of the feet that followed on the other side of the summit.

With each second the light in the east increased and though this aided their progress it would soon also reveal them.

'Speed alone will help us,' Howard exclaimed, 'I hope you're sure-footed.'

'I will try my best.'

'I know. I know.'

When Howard pointed, and tugged on the hand he grasped, Georgina felt shaken and incredulous. She gazed towards a wide river, silver white in the early dawn.

'That's the way we'll go,' he said.

'But how can we . . . ?'

His chuckle astonished her. 'That is ice, my love — a glacier. Come . . . that fellow will be breathing down our necks while you linger.'

Huge boulders fringed the glacier, with tiny rocks between that sent Georgina's feet this way and that, threatening to wrick her ankle.

'It's no use . . .' she began and saw Howard glance anxiously over his shoulder.

'It is our only hope,' he hissed, 'would you endanger both our skins by arguing?'

Mutely, she followed as, still clasping her hand in a firm grip, Howard started out across the ice.

She was venturing her first few steps across when something whizzed past her.

'Howard,' she cried, but already he was bending to touch his calf.

'Damnation!'

'What is it?'

'He's firing at us. A graze — my boot

saved the worst. But come! Quickly!' Limping, he hurried forward, dragging Georgina with him, then halted, staring down into a gap in the crystal surface.

He sighed exasperatedly. 'A fissure! And too wide for my liking. Well, there's nothing for it but we jump.'

'We cannot.'

'I can, and you will have to.'

'But . . .'

'There's no other way. And Taylor's blundering through those rocks now, soon he'll start over the ice. We can only be grateful that he's too preoccupied with keeping a foothold for firing again. Now, first I'll leap over, then you must jump towards me. I'll catch you, have no fear . . .'

No fear — when every sense was screaming that she'd be killed if she risked such folly?

Scared for his safety, biting her lip, she watched Howard leap across the chasm. He staggered a little, landing on the damaged leg, but quickly righted himself.

'Toss the baggage across,' he called, and gathered their belongings together at his feet.

'Your turn now . . .' His tone was brisk. And his arms were extended towards her.

After a deep breath, Georgina flung herself towards him.

He caught her surely, clasping her to him. She felt his heart thumping above her own.

'You see,' he said, smiling slightly.

Trembling now, Georgina let him lead her over the rest of the icy crust. Forcing herself to concentrate on the glacier's potential danger, she tried to ignore the fear of Taylor that prickled her vertebrae.

The bullet she had dreaded split the ice, sending splinters darting into her heels as she stepped on to the rocky bank.

'You'd best watch your footing instead!' Howard called back, but Taylor laughed.

'I'm not afeared,' he shouted scornfully. 'If a wench can cross this I'll not be beaten.' He fired again and his feet rasped on the icy ridges.

Howard pushed Georgina ahead, shielding her with his body as he hustled her away from the glacier.

A shot struck a rock beside their heads and Howard's fingers tightened on her shoulder. Then suddenly Taylor screamed and they heard ice cracking.

The fissure had splintered at its brink, tipping the man forward. The pistol soared from his hand to crash on to the ice, skidding away with a curious grating sound. Seth Taylor was struggling up to his shoulders now, in the cleft, yelling for assistance.

'Oh, Lord!' Georgina gasped.

'He's wedged, I reckon, only thawing ice will release him.'

'And then?'

'No man could prise himself out. The abyss appeared bottomless, his end will be mercifully swift.'

'We can't just leave him.'

'You'd see me taken prisoner first, would you?'

'No, but . . .'

'Make your choice,' Howard said brusquely.

He turned from her and ran down the rugged bank to the glacier.

'Howard!'

Not heeding her, he was crossing swiftly towards Taylor who was sinking, with only head and waving arms in sight. Howard was only a few paces from him when a despairing cry echoed back and forth among the peaks. She saw Howard staring down into the chasm, then turn from it. Her own voice felt locked within a throat frozen as the crystal river. She sobbed silently, terrified that he'd never return to her alive. And then he was stumbling towards her, head sunk into his shoulders, brows drawn fiercely together.

He said nothing as he limped up the bank,

nor when he sank on to the ground to ease off his hessian boot.

The shot had skimmed through boot and stocking, searing into the flesh of his calf where a clean wound oozed blood.

'I'll tend that.'

Georgina found clean linen in their baggage and fashioned a pad. After wiping blood from the wound she applied the pad, and tore off a linen strip, to use as bandage.

'Thank you,' he said, and caught her fingers to his lips. His blue gaze held her own for a long minute.

He lay back against a smooth rock beside her. 'You must be exhausted, I'll admit I am.'

He grew silent, moving only occasionally to ease the position of the leg. Sensing his tenseness, she was afraid he was reluctant to have her near. She had wondered before when they were alone if he thought she was playing the temptress. If he were committed to Lady Virginia whatever would he think of *her* for encouraging familiarity and . . . and much more between them! Did he believe she invited intimacies from him, as he'd implied she did from every man?

'We'll go to the nearest port where I'll see you embarked for home.'

'Howard, no!' Tears welled in her dark

eyes. So he did disapprove of her.

'Georgina, listen . . .'

'I know you warned that travelling was dangerous — and I'll admit I hadn't imagined men would try . . . I expect you've been shocked, and so have I, but I have never once encouraged their revolting advances.'

Howard laughed, as though the matter weren't grave. 'Foolish one, I only wish to protect you.'

'From myself? Would you correct my morals now?' Springing to her feet, she stared indignantly down at him. 'You'll tell me next that you're frightened I'll have you take me, against your will!'

Howard rose to face her. He pulled her against him, wanting her to recognize the need that had flared again.

'Sometimes I fear my own desire,' he said quietly, still crushing her against him.

'Is it that you're so committed to your cousin that you must deny all other women your company?'

'Lord, no.'

'Then let me be the judge of where my career shall lead me,' she said, pressing against him as if she knew he ached to know this fierce need was mutual. Her kiss was strong, and the arms, sliding within his coat to hold him more closely, no less powerful for all their slenderness.

An arm about her, Howard led her to a large rock where he drew her to him again then turned her so that her back was to the stone. He imprisoned her there with his lean body, his lips fierce on her mouth while she felt his hardness bruising her. He eased away, only to slide searching fingers within her gown, toying with her breasts until she would have cried out with the sweet sharpness of pain. But his kisses were permitting no murmur from the lips they sealed.

Georgina could not will her body to quiet and her thighs moved against his, her flat stomach thrusting closer as if to assure him that she couldn't forget the delight of loving him. Her breath was urgent, gasping, as again she slid her hands within his coat, her fingers tingling at the heat through the thinness of his shirt.

His hand left her breast to caress her smooth shoulder, then down over her back, the velvet of her gown as sensuous beneath his touch as the slender body that curved against him. His fingers travelled to her thigh, lingering there while his knee insisted that she part for him. Her legs tremored and he fondled her through the velvet.

His tongue darted between her teeth, asserting his desire, and then he was holding her only with his gaze. She shivered.

'So — it's your career, is it, that keeps you with me?' he demanded.

The russet roofs of Florence were darkened by a recent shower when the mail coach lumbered down the hill from the north; but as they reached the first few houses a watery sun emerged. Smiling, Georgina turned towards Howard.

'What a beautiful city. I'm sure only good events happen here.'

'You're romanticising again. Danger skulks in every city, as we must remember.'

As soon as the coach set them down Howard hired a carriage to whisk them away to Conte Vicenzo's home. Georgina spent most of the short journey looking over her shoulder across the river to the city, and she gasped when she saw the splendour of the place where they would stay.

'Is this really where we shall sleep?' she exclaimed as Howard assisted her from the carriage. She had glimpsed the bell tower between poplar trees but hadn't dreamed it was their destination. She gazed up now at crenellated walls, their golden stone peach-tinted by sunlight.

An aristocratic man-servant, liveried in maroon silk, was standing at the door and greeted Howard respectfully. They walked through a marble-floored hall while Crispino, the servant, addressed Howard allowing Georgina to gaze, bemused, on their surroundings.

The staircase ahead of them was wide, its balustrade looked freshly gilded. The carpeting, luxurious beneath thin soles, was of glorious colours in which crimson predominated. On the walls enormous pictures alternated with gilt-framed mirrors. At a bend in the stair, she paused, admiring the chandelier whose crystal pendants chinked in the draught fluttering its candle flames.

Georgina inhaled deeply and smiled again at Howard.

'The Conte is working in his studio,' he told her. 'We are going to our rooms and will meet him later, at dinner.'

'Working? Does the owner of this magnificent *castello* need to work?'

He smiled; glancing to the uniformed back ahead of them, he leaned towards her. 'This "magnificent" *castello* requires much upkeep. On my last visit this staircase was crumbling. Il Conte is an artist like yourself, and supplements his personal income from his paintings.'

'I wonder if he will show me some of his work.'

'I doubt it. He always appears reluctant to have friends scrutinize his craft.'

'Then I will be tactful and not mention his skill. I'd be glad, all the same, to see his work.'

Her room, to one side of the castle, had a view across the Arno swirling at its walls to the heart of Florence.

Reminding herself that in her excitement time would flit by unheeded, Georgina disciplined herself to hang garments in the heavy carved wardrobe, and placed other belongings in drawers or on the marble-topped table.

Her task completed, the room looked no more comfortable than on her arrival. And she noticed the polished floorboards were covered only with a few shabby rugs, and the window had fading curtains.

The walls too were drab, their once well-preserved panelling dull as though dried out by time. This room then must be one which had not yet been renovated.

She loved the place none the less, sensing already that its view would be a constant delight. And the huge bed, despite musty draperies, was a bed for dreaming great dreams.

She was here, at last, to draw, to do the work that had introduced her to Howard.

He implied that they'd be safe in Florence and she was happy to accept that their fears were ended. And if his alternating disclosures and reticence bewildered her, she might dismiss them. She would enjoy each facet of their stay in this picturesque *castello* and learn, if she could, to understand Howard more thoroughly.

A room for bathing adjoined her bedroom and a knock on her door brought Francesca, a maid, with gallons of heated water. Georgina luxuriated in lathering herself with tangily scented soap, rinsing away all weariness.

She dressed carefully for dinner, selecting a gown the shade of summer sea and, tying matching ribbons about her chignon, let their fronds cascade with her curls towards her face. Her eyes were brilliant with excitement, her cheeks in no need of rouge.

She was fastening a silver brooch at her low décolletage when someone knocked at her door. Opening it, she found Howard standing there.

'I thought I would escort you down to . . .' he began, and then stopped speaking while blue eyes studied first her features, then hair, before passing on to her throat then progressing to bodice, and over her gown.

He appeared to recollect himself once his

glance reached her satin toes. He cleared his throat.

'Yes. Are you ready?'

Amused, she contained a smile. 'What say you — am I suitably dressed?'

'You are beautiful, magnificent. Not the dress, Georgina, though that is exquisite, but you, yourself. You look radiant.'

She allowed herself to smile. 'Thank you.'

Georgina enquired about his leg, and learned that the servant who'd been sent to attend to the wound had declared it a superficial graze that was healing already.

She took his arm, approving his closely fitted breeches of honey-coloured cloth, the crispness of the frilled shirt with its collar points upturned to cheeks smooth from recent shaving. His waistcoat, striped in gold and green, toned with the coat of green silk whose gold buttons glinted brightly as his freshly washed hair, catching the light from a high window.

'You're a splendid escort,' she commented and saw his slight smile as they descended the staircase.

Il Conte awaited them at its foot, a striking man, fully six feet tall with shoulders a wrestler might have envied. His torso was lean, nevertheless, beneath scarlet silk waistcoat and black velvet coat. His stance was arrogant, his white breeches taut across a manly figure that seemed to thrust forward, proud of the absence of a paunch. And justly so, she mused, for a glance to aquiline features revealed him as nearing middle age.

The hair caressing his forehead was thick still, its glossy black relieved by only a dozen or so grey threads.

'Miss Morton . . .' His accented tone was warm as he reached for her fingers, and a subtle fragrance wafted to her as he bent to kiss her hand. 'You are most welcome in my home, I hope that you will find relaxation in Florence.'

As Georgina thanked him his dark gaze linked with her own before he turned aside to Howard.

'My old friend . . .' Their handclasp was firm and the Conte seemed to check emotion.

'And how was your journey?' he enquired, placing his hands on their shoulders and walking between them across the marble floor.

'Long,' Howard replied eventually, 'but that was to be expected.'

'And you, my dear,' Vicenzo said, addressing Georgina, 'were you not exhausted by it?'

'I'm thankful to be arrived here,' she responded calmly, and felt Howard's approving gaze.

She was surprised that Il Conte had no hostess at his table, although she'd had no reason to suppose he might be married. The dining-room was a delight of pale yellow walls, decorated with panels outlined by borders incorporating scarab shapes and date palms, in the fashion popularized since Napoleon's Egyptian campaign. The chairs, sofas also, beside the great fireplace were black, with fine gold lines their tasteful embellishment.

'You approve?' The count, who had seated her to his right at table, was smiling half-amused as he watched her appraisal.

'Forgive me,' she said hastily, 'I was staring.'

He touched her hand. 'The room was created to draw attention, I am pleased the intent was achieved.'

During the meal their host explained his refurbishing of the *castello*, adding that he hoped it would be completed within two years.

Howard grinned at him. 'Your paintings must be selling well!'

Conte Vicenzo's smile was wry, as if from some secret. 'Certain undertakings are reaching fruition now. But what of your own commissions?'

'The Scottish book is with the printers now. The others have sold tolerably well so far. And my publishers anticipate great demand for my guides to Europe. Since the agreement of Amiens, English people who can afford to travel are venturing across the Channel.'

Vicenzo appeared puzzled. 'Good. But I was referring to your other task, is that not proving lucrative as you anticipated?'

Howard glanced swiftly to Georgina as if to weigh her interest. Scowling, he replied in Italian.

Unable to translate, Georgina was dismayed that he excluded her so pointedly.

Howard's reply was brief, however, and their host nodded, evidently approving.

'I am pleased that you will be well paid for your information,' he said in English.

Georgina sipped her wine hastily, trying to check her agitation. Did this imply that, after all, Howard was involved in spying?

Had even their love-making been but a means of winning her trust? From the first she had wanted to believe in Howard, their weeks together had made it seem that her future was being interwoven with his. How would she bear it now if she discovered her hopes were founded on quicksand?

CHAPTER TWELVE

Tiredness ensured that Georgina slept as soon as she clambered into the outmoded bed in her room. Towards early morning, however, she awakened, tormented by her memory of Howard's words and the way she had supposed him guilty of deceit. And more than half her disturbance arose from feeling that by entertaining suspicions she was disloyal.

Restless, surrounded by the fusty draperies, she felt she would stifle. She had opened the window, but to little effect. No breeze stirred anywhere. If the atmosphere were denuded of oxygen she couldn't have felt more debilitated.

She would have crossed to the window but each limb seemed leaden, and her stomach overladen still from the rich Florentine cooking. She turned her pillow to its cooler side but now the sheet beneath her was unbearably wrinkled. She forced herself to rise from the bed.

Sighing, she went out on to the balcony to inhale the night air which appeared slightly fresher.

Florence looked beautiful still, despite her own disquiet. Stars made pinpricks in the sky as far as the horizon that was the city's encircling hills; and a waning moon gave enough light to silhouette the cathedral's dome and an assortment of towers.

The view was calming, soon she would return to sleep. A weird cry sounded, suddenly, just above her head. A sombre shape swooped past her and plummeted to the opposite river bank. Startled, her heart began pounding fiercely, out of all proportion to the slight shock.

Again, she felt the dread that Howard might, indeed, be engaged as an informer. And when she went to the bed it seemed less rather than more comfortable, and the lack of air even more intolerable. She lay in the darkness of the thick curtains and wondered how the rest of the world could slumber so readily while she remained awake.

A second strange cry seemed to echo all about the castle walls. She sighed again, suspecting she wouldn't sleep any more tonight.

A tapping noise immediately above her sent her huddling beneath the covers. Its threat, for the moment, seemed greater than that of suffocation. Reminding herself that she was supposed to be sufficiently mature to be travelling Europe, she leaned on one elbow. Listening, she detected a repetitive light drumming, rhythmic as a woodpecker . . . a sound impossible to ignore.

Finding tinder and flint, Georgina lit her candle. She slipped on the robe which seemed, in this climate, to drag on her shoulders. Putting on slippers, she took up the candle and crossed to open the door. Its hinges squealed, a noise unnoticeable in daytime. She hesitated, scarcely breathing, expecting at any moment to have every door along this corridor open on an accusatory face. Nothing happened, the very absence of movement grew sinister. She could have believed the Conte, Howard, the servants, all dead in their rooms or fled from here, so that she alone remained. In the *castello* — changed overnight from pleasant enchantment to malevolence.

Resolution calmed her panic, and strengthened shaking legs to hasten her along towards the main staircase.

She climbed as though magnetized by the knocking, almost running now, her feet silent over the thick carpeting. Abruptly, she was faced by a solid wall. Its stone was rough, as the outer walls of the castle, and equally implacable. Disbelieving that the stair led nowhere, she raised her candle until its flickering light danced her own shadow about in mockery.

Slowly, she descended, walked along to pass her own door, and continued until she reached another flight of steps. Narrow and uncarpeted, they evidently were used by servants. Trying to move quietly over each wooden tread, she began climbing.

Georgina gained a meagre corridor with ancient carpeting over dusty boards. It led to the left, with closed doors all along one wall. She hesitated, thinking to try the first handle, but the tapping continued, further away than any of these rooms.

Another stair, rising from the end of the corridor, led to an even narrower passageway, and when this turned a sharp angle she was afraid she would lose all sense of direction. But the knocking sounded clearer here, compelling her to continue.

She came to a spiral stairway, so narrow that she could touch outer and inner walls simultaneously. A draught tugged at her candle flame so that she had to shield the light.

Georgina climbed steadily without reaching either room or corridor. She was contemplating giving up when the tapping ceased. She heard the scrape of some piece of furniture, and footfalls over wooden boards. They sounded very close and she realized suddenly how difficult explaining her presence would prove.

Silently cursing her curiosity, she remained transfixed where she was. A door opened, only feet above her, and she held her breath.

But, instead of approaching, the footsteps on the stone stair receded up into the gloom. She gave a sigh of relief, steadying herself against the cold wall.

A heavy door opened and a breeze stronger than Georgina had supposed existed anywhere in Florence whirled, and fluttered out Georgina's candle.

'Oh, no!' Even the need to keep silent was neglected in the horror of being bereft of light. For some long while, Georgina stood where she was, incapable of deciding what to do. And then she started climbing, meaning to ask assistance from whoever was prowling in the night.

A few yards upwards courage drained from her. How could she admit to the inquisitive nature that had brought her up here? If Vicenzo had passed through that door how would she tell him what she had done?

Georgina ran rapidly down the stairs. Only the occasional glimmer from a slit in the thick walls gave illumination that did not reach the steps. Inevitably, she slipped on a worn stair and went tumbling, grazing herself badly. Clutching at one of the slit windows, she managed at last to check her fall.

Her heart pounding, she leaned against the wall until she had recovered. Very cautiously, step by slow step, she continued descending. All at once she was in a paved square at its foot; feeling her way around, she located a studded door. Its iron handle refused to turn, and Georgina wondered frantically how she had become trapped here. Where was the corridor from which she had emerged originally?

Steadying her rising panic she understood. Somehow, she must have missed the intersection with that corridor as she fell. Tired now and becoming increasingly bewildered, she struggled to contain tears that pricked at her eyes and tightened her throat. She pictured herself wandering night long through the *castello*, meeting no one, and only with the coming of dawn being able to find her own room.

She sighed, took a deep breath, and reminded herself that she was in no danger.

The door would not yield so she had no alternative but to climb up the way that she had come. At least mounting the stairs was less hazardous than descending. And soon she found the opening on to a corridor. Although the right-angled turning gave her a start as she blundered suddenly into its wall, it reassured her that this was indeed the route that she had first taken.

She located the wooden stair and, keeping a hand on the wall, carefully descended. Taking equal care over the rest of the way, she eventually reached what she judged to be her own corridor. But no sooner was she rejoicing over having its carpeting beneath her slippers than her heart plummeted. She was uncertain from this end which door was her own. She thought she had passed three doors when setting out, but in her eagerness to trace that tapping she'd paid all too scant attention.

Believing that she would more readily find her room from the main staircase, she continued on until she touched its gilded balustrade.

'Nearly there now,' she murmured encouragingly, resolving already never again to venture beyond her door during darkness. She was certain her room lay beyond the fourth door along. Gingerly, lest she awaken anyone slumbering beyond them, she slithered a hand over the first, second and third doors. At the fourth she turned the handle, smiling at the thought of her safe return, and pleased with the resourcefulness that had brought her here.

The door squeaked as she flung it open and she knew at once its sound was unfamiliar. About to withdraw, she began pulling the door back towards her.

'Who's there?' a male voice demanded.

Recognizing Howard, Georgina didn't know whether relief or dismay was the stronger emotion. She had not disturbed anyone else, but how might she explain to him? Indecisively, she hovered in the doorway.

He was far more adroit with tinder than she had ever been, his lighted candle was raised in one hand as he sat upright in the bed. His other hand was outstretched. She blinked; he grasped a pistol.

'Georgina.'

Devoid of speech, she clung to the door handle.

'Has no one ever taught you the courtesy of knocking?'

'I — I'm sorry.' His reproof, after the shock of learning this was not her own room, induced a strange light-headedness.

'What is it? Are you ill?'

'No, I . . . no,' she responded weakly, despite the fluttering in her chest that was making her feel most unwell.

'Then what is it?' he persisted. He left the bed, reaching for his robe and donning it swiftly as he strode towards her.

'I heard a noise.'

'Did you indeed? And has it not occurred to you that an old place like this might be subject to much creaking and rattling, to say nothing of rodents in the wainscoting or birds nesting within some crevice?'

'No, I mean . . . yes . . . You see . . .' His patent fury was making her tremble uncharacteristically. She swallowed hard, taking a deep breath, about to move into the room.

Gazing intently towards her as he crossed from the bed, Howard noticed her pallor and that she shuddered. Was she about to faint? Could he reach her before she fell?

He pulled her towards him, kicking the door to with a bare foot and holding her against himself for support. She was icy cold and he could not imagine how anyone might be so chilled in all this heat.

'You are ill, aren't you?'

She shook her head and he felt the gulp that tremored through her.

'Hush now, you're safe,' he murmured into the sweetly scented hair, his own fright already entirely dismissed.

'I am sorry,' she mumbled into his chest. 'I didn't mean to waken you, or anyone else.'

Since she had thrust open the door of his room, he could not see how she had expected to leave him undisturbed, but her distress was obvious. He awaited her explanation patiently.

She shivered and he opened his own robe, enfolding her tightly against him. Her breathing, which had been rapid and shallow, steadied and he was satisfied that faintness had been averted.

'I heard this noise,' she began, 'coming from somewhere above my head. It sounded as though someone was tapping and I couldn't get to sleep again.'

'All right, Georgina,' he said gently, 'tell me all about it in the morning.'

'Please listen, I've got to talk to somebody, I owe you some explanation. I felt I ought to find out what was causing the noise.'

'It was scarcely your affair.'

'I didn't consider that at the time! I went up the main staircase first of all, but I came to a blank wall.'

'You would — that's the limit of Vicenzo's progress with renovations.'

Georgina continued her tale, how she had

pursued the rapping sound until her candle gutted on the spiral staircase.

Howard reflected that even he'd have been reluctant to explore his friend's castle in utter darkness.

'That's how I became so confused that I found your room instead of my own.'

'You made your way back without even a candle?'

'I wondered more than once if I'd arrive before daylight.'

Now that she had revealed her story and Howard wasn't angry, Georgina's taut muscles began to relax. She was conscious immediately of the strength of this man who always seemed to reassure her. And conscious of a feeling fiercer and wilder than instilling confidence.

He was hard against her, diminishing all fear in one glorious urge to cling to him. She felt the familiar thrill of quickening pulse, and his hands moving over her back so that no part of her seemed untouched by his warmth.

She pressed into that warmth, unquestioningly, thrusting herself even more close.

Howard shut his eyes, kissing the lips which had trembled, moving him. A voice deep within him was demanding that he keep her here, that he take her to the bed.

She needed comforting, and warmth, he couldn't turn her away. Yet well he knew there'd be no checking desire if he kept her here.

Even as he contemplated sending her to her room his urgency flared into a vital throbbing, desperate for fulfilment. He stirred against her, delighting in breasts that firmed as she moved with him in a blissful unison of longing.

Her arms were around him, beneath his robe, her fingers tracing his spine, exciting, enticing, exhilarating. He sensed that in moments he'd be compelled to take her. For one further second he permitted his body to linger in this delicious proximity, and then he drew away. He sought her gaze in the candlelight. The dark eyes were like mysterious brown gems, lustrous and full of desire. He marvelled at seeing his own passion mirrored there.

Standing on tiptoe, Georgina kissed him; softly, on his cheek, but aroused as he was he could not turn coldly from her. He crushed her to him, his lips claiming hers with an intensity that surprised even himself. Georgina gave a tiny gasp and as her lips parted he felt the sharpness of her teeth on his probing tongue. When her pointed tongue began its exploration, he thrust himself against her once more, as if demanding acceptance.

She was his wife. He'd pretend no longer that this marriage had no meaning. No more could he wait with fine intentions of perfecting the life he would give her by ridding it of debts and danger. Tonight, he'd recognized anew a yearning that matched his own.

Her robe as well as his was discarded before they reached the bed. Swiftly, he removed her nightgown, his excitement increasing as candlelight flickered over the glowing white curve of her breasts. And then he was naked also, drawing her with him down on the cool sheet.

His mouth sought hers again, hungry for love, eager to end all restraint. One hand fondled her breast while the other travelled down over her flat belly.

Against his lips, she moaned when she felt his caressing fingers, and tremored at his touch. Her hand went tentatively to his thigh and then upwards. Soon passion would know no delaying. He was pressing against her now, urgent, dominating, probing between her legs until they parted readily and she felt her own body pulsing as she arched upwards. His thrusting was powerful, rhythmic, inciting her to move with him as they were joined, and though he seemed strong enough to tear her apart her own passion was no weaker.

His lips returned to hers with an urgency to echo the pressure deep within her. She slid one arm about his shoulders, her other hand went to the hair curling at his nape as if she would draw him ever closer, willing him to give.

She was scarcely aware of anything beyond sensation now; the wildness of her own desire that had her writhing beneath his weight, as if nothing would contain her joy. Her hand left his shoulders to trace the line of his spine then press at its base, clamping him hard against her. The great tide of passion sent waves coursing through her, and in them she felt the final surging for which she longed. She could not believe the wonder of belonging to him. But all too soon he grew still, and when he withdrew from her the loss she felt was more than physical. Her elation cooled swiftly and, remembering her own passion, she wondered if that had been the stronger. Had he been withholding, reluctant to give totally? Because a part of him was committed elsewhere?

Howard had risen and was slipping on his robe, telling her to do likewise.

'You must go to your room,' he said, and

read disappointment in her expression.

Silently, she left him. She was biting at her lips now instead of uttering the moans of delight that had soared through her only moments before. Dejectedly, she opened her own door. How cruelly she had learned the joy of being his wife, only to be dismissed as if she had served his purpose.

Georgina felt less wearied than she'd expected when the arrival of one of Vicenzo's maids with hot water roused her. And although she wondered still if Howard had been thinking of his cousin, she could not regret that she had shown her love for him so eagerly.

By chance they met on the stair, but by neither smile nor look did he hint that anything had occurred since the previous evening. She resolved to pretend that their lovemaking had mattered no more to her than it had to Howard.

Their host joined them at breakfast, asking after their plans and which places they would visit.

'The Duomo,' Howard told him and, glancing to Georgina, translated.

'The cathedral. And of course we'll linger over the baptistry with its magnificent doors.'

'Doors?' she enquired. 'What can be so

special about a door?'

'You will see,' Howard promised. Georgina became so mystified that when the *cabriolet* loaned by Vicenzo stopped in the Piazza San Giovanni she demanded first to see the baptistry doors.

She drew in a long incredulous breath as the morning sun glinted from their gilded carving.

'How utterly beautiful! Which superb craftsman created these doors?'

'Lorenzo Ghiberti designed and cast them with help from certain collaborators — Donatello for one.'

'You were right to call them magnificent.' Georgina gazed, entranced, at the variations of texture giving perspective to the ten scenes. 'No line drawing will do these justice.'

Howard smiled. 'Oh, come — you will exert every facet of your skill.'

But she was shaking her head. 'No, this can only be truly reproduced in colour. Have you thought to use an aquatint in your book?'

'I hadn't, no. But you might persuade me to have this particular engraving in colour, perhaps as the frontispiece.'

Georgina's brown eyes shone. 'I must attempt to reproduce this so well that all who read your book will be enraptured as I am . . .'

Howard insisted on showing her around the Duomo where Michelangelo's Pietà so moved Georgina that she longed to linger inside the cathedral's cool interior. But Howard hurried her on again.

They spent an hour walking from room to room in the Uffizi gallery, admiring works by the great masters. And when her appetite was whetted Howard took her out into the brilliant sunlight.

'The Uffizi will still be here tomorrow,' he assured her. 'And I have business that will take me away from Florence, then you may explore at will. Although I trust that you'll bear in mind that we are here to work.'

'Naturally.' She smiled. 'The sight of so much beauty makes my fingers itch to take up pen or pencil.'

A short walk brought them to the Ponte Vecchio where Georgina exclaimed delightedly.

'Shops, built on a bridge!'

'Let's stroll across and inspect their wares . . .'

Many of the shops belonged to goldsmiths. Most of the pieces displayed were exquisite and Georgina paused repeatedly to admire a beautifully fashioned brooch or jewelled ring. She particularly loved one ring, so delicately wrought that its filigree tracery reminded her of a gilded spider's web.

Howard smiled at her enthusiasm. 'You'd surely not select that rather than one set with precious stones?'

She chuckled. 'I wish I believed I might afford it.'

Howard returned with her to Vicenzo's carriage which took them up one of the surrounding hills.

'I shall want an etching of this scene of the city,' he said. 'Another spot to revisit in my absence.'

During dinner that evening Howard told Vicenzo, 'I may remain away for a night or two.'

Il Conte nodded. 'Very well.'

'Georgina has sufficient to occupy her,' Howard added, still to Vicenzo, and Georgina felt annoyed that he implied she was like some child to be amused while her elders were occupied with serious matters.

'I shall be pleased to take my time over my sketches instead of being hustled rapidly by you,' she snapped.

Surprised, Howard stared across the table but she lowered her gaze to her plate. His own appetite vanished abruptly. So she hadn't been delighted as he'd believed by all he'd shown her that day. She was, it seemed, looking forward to his absence. Perhaps she'd be glad also to keep to her own bed?

He turned to Vicenzo, who was enquiring if his business in Tuscany was similar to that which had engaged him in Portugal.

Georgina felt colour flooding her cheeks. How could the Conte embarrass him so?

When Howard responded in Vicenzo's own language she forgot the glorious day spent with her husband. Each moment of it seemed tarnished by the fear that he was never so straightforward as he appeared.

Would she never be able to follow her instinct to give him her whole heart? Would she never know what it was like to feel love unspoiled by shadows?

CHAPTER THIRTEEN

Georgina was surprised to find herself enjoying wandering about Florence without Howard. She went to the Uffizi gallery once more, not for the paintings but the view from its windows of the old Ponte Vecchio. Swiftly, she pencilled in an outline of its quaint shops.

An elderly curator with a thin face and blue eyes startled her when he paused to admire her work. But although she spoke to no one else that morning she was content.

She was driven back to the castle for luncheon but Vicenzo was working. His housekeeper, Signora Polidori, a gaunt woman who was proving more amiable than she appeared, insisted on serving a meal in the dining-room. Worried that she might be a nuisance, Georgina apologized, and was surprised when the signora laughed.

'When we have so many servants that finding work for them is a problem? No, Signorina Morton, our regret is that Il Conte spends so much time in his studio that the rest of the *castello* is rarely used.'

Having eaten, Georgina decided she was

too eager to explore the city to take the customary early afternoon rest. She had Vicenzo's coachman take her to the baptistry where she gazed again at the door which so impressed her. Pleased by Howard's promise of using an aquatint, she had purchased watercolours. Setting up her easel and finding brushes, she gave herself to enjoying the task.

It was several hours later before she gave a thought to the time. Horrified, she discovered that she had allowed herself only forty minutes for returning to the castle and preparing for dinner. Having despatched Vicenzo's *cabriolet* and doubting her ability to hire a carriage with the ease practised by Howard, she hurried through the streets, feeling very alone.

Without putting away her drawing equipment, she hastily washed face and hands in cold water, slipped on a fresh gown, and combed her curls into some semblance of order before running downstairs in a manner of which her mother would have strongly disapproved.

The Conte Vicenzo was awaiting her in the dining-room, a hand extended for her own which he pressed to his lips.

'You have had a pleasant day?'

'Most pleasant, thank you. I do love your

city — and your home, it is most kind of you to allow me to stay.'

'Not at all — how could one but be flattered by having so fair a guest.'

Il Conte appeared intent on ensuring that she did not miss Howard's company. When he had exhausted the attributes of Florence, he asked after her home and family but since he was not familiar with Kent, Georgina was at a loss to know what she might tell him.

'And you have known Howard Saunders for how long?' he enquired.

'Since January. He took me with him to Scotland to illustrate a book which he'd almost completed.'

'And your families are acquainted perhaps?'

'Oh, no.'

'Then how did you adopt this extraordinary career?'

'Extraordinary?'

'For a lady, no?'

Georgina smiled ruefully. 'So I am told. And I must confess it is rare for a young woman to take on any but the most mundane of tasks.'

Vicenzo laughed. 'Tell me — what does my friend the Lady Virginia think of your involvement with Howard?'

'I — I scarcely know.'

'She's a forcible woman, with the beauty to ensure her own desires.'

'I am sure.'

'But you do not approve.'

'I'm sorry, I didn't wish to show disapprobation. She is your friend.'

Again, the Conte laughed. 'And has been for many years. If it weren't for the certainty that she and Howard will eventually make a match, I would have courted her myself.' Wryly, he glanced about the room. 'And if I had, her wealth would have restored my home much more speedily.'

Georgina wondered if his interest in Virginia Mayburn had prevented Vicenzo marrying elsewhere, and then the meal ended. He excused himself as the servants came to clear away.

Georgina went to her room but found she could not settle. The agony of not being able to express her love for Howard! Hoping to dismiss her dread of a life in which he, it seemed, would have no part, she determined to take advantage of the Conte's invitation to explore his home. She had been intrigued by the castle from the moment of her arrival and would take time now to learn more of its delights.

She went down the stairs, passed the

dining-room door and opened the one next to it to find herself in the drawing-room. Once exquisite, its walls now were dulled, its silver chandelier lustreless, the matching candelabra tarnished. A sad, neglected room, she thought, and imagined some lady of the house superintending its renovation, restoring life to the once beautiful decor. The curtains would be replaced by fresh velvets or brocades in brilliant colours, to draw the eye towards the fine windows. The furniture would be waxed thoroughly to restore its gleam, and the large mirror over the marble mantel polished until it reflected back the satisfying scene. Yes, a woman could do much here, even without Lady Virginia's capital. Although, Georgina mused, wouldn't it be excellent if Vicenzo established his old friend as mistress here?

'You're an idiot,' she chided herself, 'painting rainbows in shadows by pretending there is any way Howard will not discard you for his cousin.'

Sighing, she went out, closing the door behind her. There seemed no alternative to returning to her room. It was evident Howard was not coming back tonight, she must prepare for solitude. She must also accept the disappointment of not seeing him before she slept. Already, she longed to hear his voice, to see the wry amusement and warmth in his glance. How could she have grown dependent upon a man so attractive that the most exotic woman alive would be flattered by a smile, while she with no outstanding feature could not hope to hold his interest?

In the corridor as she approached her room Georgina heard the tapping sound that had alerted her during her first night. She felt she dared investigate in daylight, but equipped herself with candle, tinder and flint.

She began following the route previously explored and all the while the noise grew more distinct. When she reached the spiral stair she was certain her search was ending. And she felt equally sure that the Conte, so agreeable over dinner, would welcome a fellow artist if she came to his studio.

She reached the door from which he'd emerged and knocked on its heavy timber. She knocked again when she'd evoked no response, feeling irritated by being ignored by whoever was making that strange insistent tapping sound. Slowly, she opened the door.

Il Conte was sitting at an easel, his brush darting swiftly over a canvas, while his dark gaze flitted just as quickly between the picture on which he worked and another that stood on a second easel, to one side. Still, he appeared oblivious of her, and for the present Georgina was content to admire the dexterity with which he applied colour. Eventually though, embarrassed by her feeling of intrusion, she spoke.

'Hello, Vicenzo. You did say that I might take a look around . . .'

'*Si?*' he snapped and half-turned towards her. 'I did not mean that you should intrude here.'

Georgina said nothing.

'Well?' His dark eyes looked black in the north light from the enormous window, which had evidently replaced an original more in keeping with the rest of the castle.

'Being an artist, I naturally was interested.'

He swung round on the stool and began painting again, even more rapidly, as if to dismiss her. 'Would you leave . . .'

It was a command rather than a question. His determination to have her out increased Georgina's resolve to learn its reason. Vicenzo seemed to forget her as he concentrated. Her gaze was drawn from the flying brush to further slight movement. As he worked, an elegant foot tapped rhythmically against the base of the easel.

Georgina smiled to herself. She had solved the mystery of the noise that she'd heard.

'Has deafness afflicted you?'

'No, I . . . may I not simply watch?'

Vicenzo sprang away from the easel, dislodging the canvas. Yelling one of the Italian oaths that she'd heard often in the city streets, he grabbed at the canvas before it reached the floor. Carefully, he replaced it on the easel, inspecting minutely for any marring of wet paint. And then he turned, strode to her, and seized both her shoulders.

Georgina gasped, afraid he would hurl her from the room. He was only fractionally less violent. Fiercely, he shook her, lifting her feet from the floor.

'Get out of here, out . . . out . . . !'

She seemed to drop on to her feet when he released his hold. Struggling to check her dizziness, she fled towards the door. As she chased down the spiral steps she heard his voice following.

'Out . . . out . . . *out!*' Sounding like some fiend.

Georgina sat, quivering, on the bed in her room. Dared she stay the night in this castle with only his servants to protect her from Vicenzo's temper? If Howard were here she would suggest that they find other accommodation. But then if he were here she would not have sought the Conte's company — nor would have investigated strange sounds on her own.

She would tell Howard when he returned. Until then she must calm herself so that sleep might help the hours to pass. Darkness was falling now; she couldn't imagine feeling safe anywhere but in this bed.

Vicenzo had seemed a devil, snarling his dismissal, and now she cowered as from some supernatural force. She reminded herself of his courtesy, of his interest in her own work, but when she slept it was to waken frequently, hearing the tapping sound, and feeling no less disturbed now that she knew its source.

She rose as the sun appeared over the hills, and prayed that Howard might have returned. He was not at breakfast, but nor was Vicenzo, sparing her that particular confrontation. She would collect sketching equipment and palette, make for the baptistry, and try to forget her apprehension by continuing her painting.

Signora Polidori saw Georgina leaving and the two women chatted about the delight of going out while the streets remained comparatively cool.

'I am so eager to see everything,' Georgina admitted, 'that I venture out when those who live here would stay indoors.'

A voice behind intervened, 'And that is foolish.' Georgina started, and shuddered when Il Conte placed a hand on her shoulder. But when she dared turn and glance up he was smiling.

'We cannot have you affected by too much sun, can we now?' he said. 'I would hate you to be unwell.'

She did not understand; he might have been a different person from the one who'd raged at her the previous evening. She could almost believe the incident a trick of her imagination.

Despite his changed manner, however, she felt uneasy in his company, and saying that she had much to accomplish that morning, she went out.

The great baptistry doors looked just as wonderful as before and soon Georgina was totally committed to capturing their splendour. Yesterday she had outlined their shape and sketched in each panel, trying to achieve correct perspective. Today she would begin detailing the design of the relief.

Her favourite scene, to which her gaze slid repeatedly, depicted Jacob and Esau, and she had to discipline herself to giving equal attention to the rest.

The morning was passing swiftly. So enthralled was she by her task that Georgina was unaware of being watched. Presently, she sensed someone standing scrutinizing her drawing.

'A touch more emphasis on the creation of Adam and Eve, I think . . .'

'Howard!' Swinging round on her folding stool, Georgina's pleasure at seeing him was shining in her eyes.

Lord, he thought, is this radiant creature smiling for me! He smiled back.

'Don't let me distract you.'

She laughed. 'A moment ago I'd have said no one could.'

'I'll leave you in peace then . . .'

'No.' As he half-turned from her, Georgina caught his hand.

'Is anyone expecting you to eat at the *castello*?' he asked.

'Nothing was mentioned, but Signora Polidori had a meal ready for me yesterday.'

'Then it would be discourteous to remain outdoors. And I suppose I ought to caution you against sitting in the noonday heat.'

'I've been warned already, by Vicenzo.' His name brought to mind their disagreement, and how frightened she'd been.

'Georgina — what is it? Is the sun too strong already?'

'No. No, I . . . it is nothing.' She turned away, collecting together her equipment.

'You may as well tell me. I'm determined to learn what has upset you.'

'I'll tell you as we go . . .'

For some time Georgina said nothing, but as they walked along the streets crowded with brightly-clothed citizens, she told him briefly of her visit to the Conte's studio and his reaction.

Howard sighed. 'I did warn you, didn't I, against trespassing there?'

'Yes, but . . .'

'But what? Georgina, it is his home and we are fortunate indeed to be staying there. We must respect his wishes.'

'I don't understand though why we have to keep out of that particular room.'

'You don't need to understand,' he told her curtly. 'You must simply accept it.'

Although Georgina would still have preferred to find somewhere else to stay, it appeared that the atmosphere at the castle was again amiable. Conte Vicenzo joined them for luncheon and included her in their conversation, thereby implying his forgiveness.

Howard seemed elated by his excursion into the Tuscan hills. By the end of their meal Georgina was wondering how she could have contemplated leaving such a pleasant household.

Returning with her to the baptistry, Howard remarked that he supposed she would be reluctant to concentrate on other illustrations until this one was completed. He stayed at her side taking notes, and then excused himself. He appeared to expect her to question him; but content to be left to her work, Georgina was also aware of his desire for privacy.

When he reappeared she noticed that he smiled readily, but she still refrained from quizzing him. Her preliminary watercolour of the baptistry doors wasn't yet finished, but she was dissatisfied with her efforts to reproduce their splendour.

'This is where you employ self-discipline,' Howard told her. 'Put this from your mind while you're engaged in something else that I require of you.'

'Yes, but . . .'

'I believed you were going to show me how efficient you could be.' His voice was chill with reproof and she wondered what had whisked away his good humour.

'And so I will,' she rejoined sharply.

Howard did not answer, but as they walked towards the Ponte Vecchio she caught the gleam of amusement in eyes that shone blue as the Arno. The man was baiting her. Provoking her.

When they returned to the castle Signora Polidori greeted them in the great entrance hall, saying awkwardly that her master was continuing with his work and asked that they excuse him from the evening meal.

'He is bad host to you, I fear,' she said, frowning, 'though in admitting so I most likely risk my position here.'

'Do not fret, signora,' Howard responded warmly. 'Miss Morton and I will find each other's company congenial enough.'

Georgina concealed a smile. Since his return Howard certainly seemed as well-disposed towards her as she might have dared to hope. And if, for the one evening, she wished to pretend that no Lady Virginia existed to prevent their relationship strengthening, where would be the harm?

She dressed carefully in a gown of ivory-coloured satin whose skirt was decorated with a deep band of embroidery to complement similar trimming enhancing the low décolletage. She loved the classical styles currently in vogue, aware that their slender lines accentuated her slight figure, and that her breasts were sufficiently full to draw admiration without appearing indelicate.

This evening she paid particular attention

to her hair, brushing until its sheen lightened by the sun, looked like burnished mahogany.

Her cheeks flushed in anticipation of an evening to be spent tête-à-tête with Howard, she needed no rouge to beautify them. And the dark tendrils that caressed her temples emphasized the gleam in her eyes.

Slowly, she descended the stair to find Howard crossing swiftly from the dining-room. He had evidently been listening for her tread; he extended a hand, waiting until she slid her fingers into his grasp.

He also had dressed with care. She admired the pale breeches neatly cladding slim hips and firm thighs. His coat was of a dark blue silk and his eyes reflected its shade as their gaze appraised her entire person. Her hand was drawn to his lips and she felt the tremor which always accompanied his touch.

He said nothing, yet his silence was more reassuring than any words he might have chosen, and the absolute approval in his expression sent a quiver coursing through her. An arm about her, he led her through to dinner.

'I am pleased you have returned,' she said presently, without consciously deciding to reveal her pleasure.

Howard smiled, but continued eating the pasta set before him as though absorbed in the movement of fork from plate to lips and back again.

It was only when they had strolled from the dining-room to the garden that Howard acknowledged her admission.

'You were not sorry then to have me supervise your work again?' he enquired, studying her as he leaned nonchalantly against the wall separating garden from the river.

Georgina smiled. 'You are not, after all, proving too arduous a task master!'

'Do I have your word then that you'll remain with me?'

'You wish my assurance that I shall accompany you to Rome? Is it that important? If so you have my promise now . . .'

'Do you think I care that much to have your illustrations?'

Georgina flushed, she had presumed too much. 'I am sorry, you must choose, of course, the person who'll accompany you.'

'I have chosen. Some while ago.'

She looked down, wondering how to respond now, when it seemed a whole arena of half-formed dreams was proffered for her approval.

'I had hoped, but . . .'

'Yes?'

She swallowed then inhaled deeply. 'They say that you will one day wed Lady Virginia.'

'Do *they?* That, my love, will never happen. The last thing I intend is making her mistress in *my* home.'

'I see.'

'Do you? Do you really see, Georgina, where this leads us?'

'I — I believe so.'

He took her right hand and slipped upon its third finger a ring taken from his pocket. Without releasing her hand, he gazed passionately into her eyes. And then his lips claimed her own, fervently, while the hardness of his lean body told of his feelings. The familiar pulsing sent a dizziness to her head, and made her yearn to draw ever closer in his arms.

Without another word he released her. Glancing down she saw the ring was the one she'd so admired in the shop on the Ponte Vecchio. But why had he placed it on her right hand instead of left? And why did he say so little of what this meant? Was he merely buying her?

CHAPTER FOURTEEN

For several days they scoured Florence for every place that should be included in the guide Howard was writing. Georgina sat sketching while he was making notes, only returning to the castle for meals and to sleep. She scarcely thought now of the alarm she had felt within the stout walls of that lovely building. With Howard her constant companion, she remained unsusceptible to its atmosphere which often seemed so mysterious.

Some days they saw Vicenzo only briefly and always he was courteous. Georgina soon ceased to wonder even if he were restraining his annoyance with her, on account of Howard's presence.

One week after Howard had given her the ring, Georgina noticed, returning for dinner, that her shoes were dusty and the hem of her gown was soiled by the walking they had done. She was afraid she had begun to pay too little attention to her appearance, which seemed unfair to her escort. Howard always appeared immaculately groomed. She would not have him think her careless of her looks.

After bathing, she dressed in a blue satin gown with lace trimming of the same shade in a deep band at its hem, and a matching lace overtunic culminating in a flattering low neckline. Finding a satin ribbon of similar blue, she tied her curls so that they framed her face.

Signora Polidori told them that Vicenzo was again excusing himself in order to work. Georgina felt Howard's gaze on her as he thanked the housekeeper and suggested she send in their first course.

Whenever she and Howard dined alone, Georgina secretly fantasized that they were in their own home, being attended by their own servants. Although if that had been so tonight she'd have reprimanded the liveried man whose lewd stare went so often to her décolletage.

Howard began discussing Napoleon's current campaigns as if he respected her opinion on important matters, and Georgina felt utterly content. They went afterwards to the drawing-room where he opened the file where he kept his notes. They had decided to plan which area of the city they would visit on the following day.

Two or three papers slid on to the carpet and, falling near her feet, Georgina retrieved them. About to hand them across, she saw that they were maps and the uppermost was headed 'Tuscany'. She asked if the map showed somewhere that they would explore.

'I have been there already,' Howard stated coldly, snatching the maps.

'Was this why you went off on your own?'

'And if it was . . . ?' he demanded, his tone dangerously taut.

Now that it was already too late Georgina decided to ask no further questions.

Howard sighed. 'Georgina, you have an infuriating habit, sometimes, of conducting an inquisition as though I were incapable of deciding the merit of my own actions.'

'No, I . . .'

He interrupted by rising angrily from his chair. 'I say that you have, madam! Time and again you question me. I have never accounted for my behaviour, and will not be called to such account by any woman!'

'My dear Howard, I did not intend that you should feel anything of the kind!'

'No? Then you've a fine way of leaving me to mind my business!'

'Howard, please. I am sorry to have caused this trouble.'

'And I am sorry — I thought we were learning to understand one another. Instead of which, I see you know nothing about me at all.'

'I was wrong and I apologize, can you not forget . . .'

'I wish I could. But each time you put me through this cross-questioning you have me wondering how in the world I can endure another day of it!'

'I do see how you must feel, but can't you see how this has come about? You know how alarmed I was when Taylor and Roberts pursued you all the way to the Alps.'

'So that is it. I feared as much. How many times have I told you, Georgina, that I am innocent of all treachery?'

She could not speak. A lump had risen in her throat and her eyes smarted with tears that she swore would not be shed.

'You still doubt me,' he stated coldly. 'I'd have thought that you, Georgina, might have accepted my word.'

'I do want to,' she mumbled, 'oh, so much I want to. Don't you understand how important it is to me to believe in you?'

'That comes well from you, madam, when you tricked your way into my employment, signing your work as a man! You easily overlook your own tendency towards deception!'

'That was nothing of the kind.'

'And nor is this, but I doubt I'll ever convince you.'

'Of course you will — and could do so immediately if you would explain . . .'

'Explain! Don't you know that I need you to trust me? And that trust is rooted in having such faith in another that one doesn't seek explanations.'

'Very well. I will curb my tongue — you have my word that never again will I trouble you with questions.'

Howard snorted. 'And there's a fine compliment, if you please! "I will curb my tongue." Not because you believe in me but because you know questions irk. No, Georgina, that will not do! There'll be nought between us while you are this mistrustful.'

'I do believe in you, I . . .'

He turned from her and began thrusting the papers into his file.

'You have shown me to the contrary, I'd be only too delighted to have you demonstrate otherwise. Meanwhile, you're a tolerable artist, I suggest you concentrate on something that is within your powers.'

'Howard . . .' She came up behind him to catch at his sleeve, dreading that he might leave this unpleasantness between them.

He shrugged away her hand. 'You'd best learn diplomacy if no other grace. Let me alone now. We're neither of us in a humour that would improve matters could we command the entire English language!'

Georgina ran up to her room, longing for privacy. Out of breath, she leaned against the door once she was safe inside, determined that even here her tears would remain unshed. But most distressing of all was her sudden realization that nothing that Howard might have done could alter her love for him.

It was almost dark now beyond the window, the last trace of red and purple merging with the night clouds. Miserably, she crossed to draw the curtains, pausing to glimpse the cathedral dome, reminded of Howard's attunement with her while they explored the city. Would they ever regain that compatibility?

Without lighting the candle, she went to lie on the bed, neglecting to undress, caring not at all if she lay all night long in the fine gown which should have earned his admiration.

Stifling though the room was, she pulled the bed curtains past her head as though she might exclude everyone from the ache that now caused her temples to throb.

She had lain for some while, too miserable even for thinking, when her opening door aroused a sudden exhilaration. *He* was coming to her! Knowing his criticism to be unwarranted, he came now to apologize. Already she imagined them rushing together in an ecstacy of conciliation. A thrill tremoured through her limbs.

'Howard . . .'

The soft footfalls halted just the other side of the bed hangings. Someone was breathing rapidly; a man . . . yet not Howard.

Georgina swallowed, apprehension bringing perspiration to her palms. A shiver scaled her spine. She waited . . . waiting seemed like infinity. And all she could hear was this swift intaking and exhalation of breath. Was this one of the servants — the man perhaps whose lewd gaze had examined her décolletage?

Or was it . . . ? Maybe she had been right and this was Howard, coming not in contrition but with intent to . . . What would he do to her? There was one sure way of asserting himself.

And yet, while she was supposing he might have come to show her who was master, the breathing stirring the curtain at her head revealed menace rather than sensuality.

She could bear the suspense no longer. 'Howard?'

The laugh was harsh, and familiar, though not Howard's.

She felt the weight as someone sat upon the edge of her bed and tried to move away, but a firm thigh trapped her skirt.

Again, the intruder laughed. 'Ah — so. It is trysting-time, no? And I have learned what keeps my friend Howard gazing with those brilliant blue eyes upon his little artist. I am so happy for him that he suffers no frustration.' Vicenzo's chuckle shook the bed.

Recovering slightly, Georgina extricated her gown and rose.

'Vicenzo, I did not expect that you'd come creeping to my room. Isn't this abusing a host's privilege?'

His laughter was quieter, its amusement reassuring. 'My poor Georgina, you're too cynical about the motivation of the male of the species . . .'

Exasperated, she sighed. 'Perhaps. But I do not believe I am obliged to entertain you at this hour.'

Vicenzo's silence seemed furtive. She had found her candle though, and tinder and flint. The flickering light revealed him holding her portfolio.

'That is mine,' she snapped.

All humour drained from him, and he looked threatening.

'I suppose you meant to return this without my knowledge.'

His stare was calculating as he dropped the folder on to the bed.

'I cannot lie. A fellow artist, I was interested to see your work. *You* should understand that incentive.'

Georgina said nothing. Several drawings had slithered from the portfolio; handling them respectfully, he glanced through them.

'You're very adroit with your pen, pencil as well. Have you never thought to let your craft earn for you?'

'It does — you don't suppose I work unpaid for Howard Saunders?'

'I'm sure he pays for all your . . . services. But I mean more money than you would ever have dreamed of . . .'

'I have sufficient to give me the kind of life I wish, enabling me to travel.'

'No, Georgina, no — I mean so much wealth that everyone will see you've made more with your craft than any man. Any, that is, excepting myself.'

'You are wasting your time. I work with Howard.'

'Work with me also.'

'No, no.'

'You refuse? Think, *cara*, what I offer.'

Shaking her head, Georgina collected her drawings into the folder and shut them away in a cupboard.

'I am tired, would you please take your leave of me.'

Approaching her from behind, he seized her wrist. She trembled, terrified he'd use force on her. He swung her round to face him.

'I propose that you lend me your skill, for you would not enjoy the alternative.'

'No threat will make me change my mind.'

'None? Ha! Your friend Howard Saunders is in constant danger of arrest. You know that, and I know the reason. One word, and our authorities here would hand him to English loyalists who hound him the breadth of Europe. He would be hanged.'

'You are bluffing.' She struggled to free herself of the hand biting into her wrist.

'You are mistaken, Georgina.'

'Howard would do nothing dishonest,' she stated, and wished she had felt this certainty when she was actually with her husband.

'My dear girl, do you suppose they would continue to pursue him as they have, without proof of his guilt?'

'There can be no truth in the rumours,' she insisted.

He let go her wrist. 'We shall see, *cara*, we shall see. But would it not be better if you weren't dependent upon him? If some . . . mischance removed him you would be incapable of supporting yourself.'

'There are other people who require illustrators.'

'Possibly. But there are easier means of earning your living with pen or pencil.'

'Then *if* the time came for me to do so I would be grateful for your advice.'

Il Conte nodded, pensively, gazing down. He seemed to dismiss the matter and was smiling when he raised his dark eyes to her own.

'You would be too busy even to attempt a leisure time experiment?'

'Experiment?'

'With your pen, Georgina, with your pen. This would be copying merely, for someone with your skill a few hours' work.'

'Doing what?'

'In the Uffizi gallery there is a drawing Leonardo da Vinci made in preparation for painting The Adoration of the Kings. I challenge you to make a copy of it.'

'But why?'

'To prove that an accurate reproduction of it is within your capabilities. And to assert your independence.'

'You mean someone would want to buy such a copy?'

'Providing it's as good as I expect, I will find you a buyer.'

'Well, perhaps I will.'

'Be sure and show me the result,' Vicenzo said, smiling.

When he had left Georgina found her confidence returning. Vicenzo had been kind, expressing belief in her ability; she might try to copy the drawing.

As the Conte left her room Howard was coming upstairs.

'Did Miss Morton send for you?' he enquired icily.

Vicenzo frowned. 'You should know by now that no one sends for me.'

'But had she asked that you visit her room?'

Vicenzo smiled. Displeased, Howard inhaled sharply, his nostrils flaring.

'I would have a private word with you if I may.'

Still smiling, Il Conte led him along the corridor and into the library. He indicated a comfortable chair, offered Howard a drink which was refused, and poured brandy for himself.

'*Si* . . . ? So you were concerned for Miss Morton. And would not have an old rake like myself in contact with her? Then be assured, it was a matter of business that took me to her, no more than that.'

'Business?'

'As one artist to another. But tell me, what of your plans?'

'They need time . . . My cousin, the Lady Virginia, has substantial wealth, and when my own parents died impoverished Sir Jonathan — Lady Virginia's father — became my guardian.'

'I knew nothing of this — but is there reason that I should?'

'Only that you might understand my relationship with Georgina. I wish the world to know of my desire to claim her as my bride. But I have debts to settle. When Virginia inherited on Sir Jonathan's death, she was the only one I could turn to for support.'

'Ah.'

'She was not ungenerous. Whatever faults she might possess miserliness is not one of them. She financed my early journeys when I began writing travel books. She's always refused to accept piecemeal settlement, but monies have been accruing over the years. Recently I travelled under a commission for which I received advance payment. I am at last, able to discharge the entire debt.'

'So, you will be free of Virginia. And what of her . . . ?'

'What do you mean?'

'Oh come, Howard — it is common knowledge that she's had her eye on you since you were fondling together behind her father's back.'

'That is over,' Howard snapped.

Vicenzo laughed. 'As you will. And it does me no harm that you and Virginia should call an end to any dallying. You'll go to London then to settle with her?'

Howard shook his head. 'She is here now, in Venice.'

As Howard passed Georgina's door he hesitated, but then he knocked. Unaccustomed though he was to explaining his actions, he must reassure her and tell her how he'd soon be rid of his cousin.

When she opened to him Georgina was wearing a robe which she seemed to have donned hastily.

'Were you sleeping?'

She shook her head, her gaze reproachful. 'Did you suppose that I would be?'

'Georgina, may I come in?'

'I think not.'

'But I wish to talk with you.'

'Does your remaining there, prevent your doing so?'

'No.'

'If the matter is of interest perhaps you

would reveal it, and then you may go.'

'Very well.' She was being childish and they both knew it. 'I am leaving for Venice in the morning, and will be away for one day, maybe two. My cousin is staying there and . . .'

'You mean that wom . . . Lady Virginia?'

'Yes.'

'So you're running to her, just because everything I say does not happen to please you!'

'I am going for one reason only . . .' Howard began quietly.

Georgina interrupted sharply. 'I don't care what you do, I seek no explanations from you.'

'Georgina, don't . . .'

The door was closed against him so that he was left standing alone and raging in the corridor.

CHAPTER FIFTEEN

The tears that Georgina had restrained that evening saturated her pillow when she thought of Howard's words. He was going to Virginia Mayburn. Her sobbing penetrated the wall to his room so that he was tired and irritable when he rose at dawn to prepare for the journey.

The knowledge that Georgina was a headstrong girl who had not yet acquired the habit of listening before flying to conclusions was of no consolation. An endearing trait it may well be at times, but that did nothing now to dispel the unease with which Howard left for Venice.

Determined not to appear distressed, Georgina was pale but composed during breakfast with the Conte. And if chatter alone could reassure him that all was well with her, her ceaseless gossip might have suggested excellent spirits.

Breakfast ended, she went to her room and started packing her belongings. She had decided that Howard should return to Florence to find her *en route* for England. If she had misjudged his purpose in visiting Virginia he was acquainted with her home beside Knole Park. Her mood was such that she could determine that her home was the only place that he would find her.

It was only when she had completed packing that Georgina realized that she hadn't sufficient money to take her twenty miles, much less all the way to England. All her expenses had been paid by Howard! And she had requested that he pay for her work only at the end of the assignment. In this way she had thought to avoid the risk of the monies being lost or stolen.

She stood gazing out across the Arno, wondering how on earth she could raise enough to cover the cost of her homeward journey and accommodation along the route. She found she was toying with the gold ring that Howard had given her. A lump rose in her throat. Whatever became of her, she could not part with Howard's token. The ring would remain on her finger even though she were never to see him again.

Sighing bleakly, she turned to her portfolio, wondering if she might perhaps execute drawings for other writers, but she was aware that such a commission would take far longer than she wished to spend in Florence. Seeing her own work, however, reminded her of Conte Vicenzo's suggestion. Why shouldn't she attempt a copy of the Leonardo drawing which he had mentioned? She had not believed that she would be obliged to comply so soon, but if his claim were true and she could earn some money this could be her one chance for quitting the city.

Georgina gathered together her drawing equipment and hurried from the castle. It was early still, and cooler than the weather to which she had grown accustomed here. Her step was swift, as she made her way through the streets leading to the Uffizi gallery and her arrival coincided with the opening of its doors.

Pleased that she would have time to commence her copy of the sketch before the gallery filled with sightseers, she passed from room to room in search of the Leonardo drawing that Vicenzo had described.

Finding it took several minutes and immediately Georgina's spirits plummeted. It was far more intricate than she remembered, and had evidently been drawn by Leonardo da Vinci as he thought out the complete composition of the picture. Some lines were superimposed upon others as if he had made alterations but no deletions.

Numerous lines ran from the foreground into the distance and she would manage well enough, to reproduce these; but then there were figures, some human, some of horses, and many of them were incomplete. Where in the world would she begin copying such a multitude of forms?

With a sigh, Georgina set up her folding stool, got out paper and pencils and began the daunting task.

When it was time for luncheon she had no appetite, upset still by her difference with Howard before his departure to join his cousin. Leaving the Uffizi only to find something to quench her thirst, she was absent scarcely ten minutes. On returning she found she was delighted by her copy which, even to herself, appeared scarcely discernible from the original. At least the Conte should be pleased with her — she hoped he'd be true to his word and ensure that she earned well from her day's work.

She had the drawing completed except for a camel which she had left because of the difficulty of portraying so unfamiliar an animal. Her head was aching, her eyes smarting from concentrating so hard, and her fingers were numb with holding her pencil. Struggling to make her reproduction lifelike, she sensed someone was watching her.

Pencilling in the last few lines of the beast's head, she did not turn immediately.

A voice spoke behind her and she swung round with a smile.

'You are talented indeed, I see now that professional interest brings you again to our gallery,' said the old curator whom she had met previously.

'Thank you,' she responded, grateful for his approval. 'I am pleased that you do not think my time has been wasted.'

'Wasted!' The old man chuckled, the blue eyes warming and sharp features softening with his smile. 'You've a rare skill, madam, would that I had half your craftsmanship.'

'You also draw then?'

'Once, I drew — painted as well, but with the years I have learned to accept that my talent is limited. Yours is not. You've had tuition, of course?'

'In England — from Professor Anstey, though he taught topographical illustration rather than copying.'

'And perhaps to amuse yourself by attempting to copy a master?'

Georgina smiled. 'I was issued a challenge, by our host in Florence.'

'I'll wager he'll be astounded by the result. You've exceptional skill, and courage to try something so difficult.'

The old curator left Georgina to add the finishing touches to her drawing before the gallery closed for the day.

As one of the servants was entering the dining-room with their first course that evening, Georgina began telling the Conte about her work.

Vicenzo frowned, and she dreaded that he had not been serious when making the suggestion. His eyes were on the servant's back, however, and when the door closed on the man Vicenzo turned to her.

'I make a practice of discussing my affairs only when servants are absent. You must forgive my insisting that you do likewise.'

She wanted to protest that she had not taken this matter so gravely. But she realized that if she intended earning from her experiment, she would do better to remain silent.

'You say you have copied the Leonardo,' he continued, 'surely you cannot mean that the drawing is already completed?'

'Oh, yes. But I have worked all day long at the task.'

'And you have the work in your room?'

'Yes. Should I have brought it down with me?'

Vicenzo shook his head. 'We will take the drawing to my studio when we have eaten.

The light there is better.'

She was astonished that he now intended admitting her to the room where he had so objected to her intrusion, but when he led the way up the staircase and waited for her to collect the sketch the Conte appeared so amiable that she supposed agreeing to make the copy had increased his respect for her talent.

He closed the studio door and went over to the long window whilst she opened her portfolio and took out the drawing. Even now her sketch's similarity to Leonardo da Vinci's startled her, and she felt a glow of pride at finding herself capable of producing so intricate a piece of work.

Feeling embarrassed and unsure of what to say, she simply crossed to Vicenzo and handed the paper to him.

He drew in a sharp breath and stared intently at her sketch, his dark eyes first narrowing then gradually widening.

'You did this?' he enquired. 'Unaided?'

She nodded. 'As you bade me. As an exercise.'

'Exercise!' he interrupted. 'Dear God, the girl presents so fair a facsimile and she calls the work an exercise!' He placed a hand on her shoulder while he gazed from her face to the drawing he held, then back again to her.

'I hardly believed when I asked you to attempt this that I entertained a genius beneath my roof. I . . . you'll be rich, Georgina, if this is a sample of your art.'

'But I don't want . . .'

'Not want? Do not tell me you'd prefer working for Saunders for a pittance now — I'll not credit that.'

'Maybe not, but . . .'

'But nothing! Work with me, *cara*, and together we'll become so wealthy that you'll be paying the likes of Saunders.'

'You do not understand.' About to reveal her decision to leave Florence at once, she checked herself. Perhaps it were wiser to secure her means of departing first.

'You like the drawing then?' she asked.

'Like?' Il Conte chuckled. 'You'll soon see how well liked this little sketch will be.'

'Good,' Georgina replied swiftly, 'for I am in need of money at once, and so will be grateful if you can find a buyer promptly.'

He appeared disconcerted. 'A buyer?'

'You gave me to understand that you could obtain a fair price.'

Sensing his reluctance to discuss a financial arrangement, Georgina wondered if Vicenzo now had in mind a different scheme. Well, if her reproduction were that outstanding, she might obtain better payment elsewhere. The old curator at the Uffizi could know of someone who'd appreciate the copy that he praised. She prepared to slip the drawing into her portfolio.

'I'll not take up any more of your time.'

'Wait.' In a few swift strides Vicenzo was at her side, his grasp on her fingers iron-hard.

'You say you need money?'

Georgina nodded. 'And I am not prepared to wait.'

'In that case I will serve friendship by making you an offer. But once you accept payment you must understand that you have no further claim upon me for possession of the sketch.'

'That is understood,' she agreed, wondering why he was so determined to obtain sole rights to the drawing.

'And you'll not object if you later learn that I've made a profit from my investment?'

Georgina laughed. 'I don't see how you would, but I'll be pleased for you if you do. All I want now is sufficient money for my immediate needs.'

The Conte's dark eyes scrutinized her sharply. 'Surely Saunders is keeping you?' and then he smiled. 'You will soon be solvent again, do not worry.'

He went to a safe over in one corner, took

a key from his watch chain, and unlocked the door.

'Here.' Locking the safe again, he crossed back to Georgina and, after taking the drawing from her unresisting fingers, began counting out a heap of banknotes. Even allowing for her lack of familiarity with the local currency, Georgina was aware that it was a large sum of money. Surely it was too much? Only the thought of the journey that she planned, and her need to be prepared for any emergency, held her silent.

Quietly, she thanked him as she gathered together the pile of bank notes.

'And you'll do more work like this for me, will you not?' Vicenzo asked. 'Now you have learned it brings rewards.'

'I — I . . .' She gulped down her admission that she would be leaving the city just as soon as she had reserved a seat in a northbound coach.

'As long as I remain in Florence I shall be pleased to do so.'

The Conte would have kept her company for the rest of the evening but Georgina was exhausted by the tedious work that had followed her restless night. In her room she took out her belongings which, readypacked, she had concealed from any inquisitive gaze. Tucking the banknotes in among her clothing, she smiled slightly. Distressed she might be by Howard's behaviour, but she found some consolation in her own ability to take care of her return to England. Tomorrow she would leave and nothing or no one on this earth would prevent her.

Georgina left the castle even earlier on the following morning. She did not take her possessions, intent on first securing a seat for the journey. She walked quickly towards an inn where she had seen a coach taking up passengers for the route over the Brenner Pass.

The inn resembled many that she had seen in England, with an archway leading through to a large courtyard. The mail coach had just departed and the yard was, for the moment, deserted.

She was gazing towards the door, trying to remember the necessary Italian phrases, when a hand thumped on to her shoulder.

Startled, she gasped.

'Don't make a fuss, lady, and maybe you'll go unharmed.' The voice was English and, worse, one that she recognized. Georgina had no need to turn to identify the one person whom she had most dreaded meeting.

'I see that you remember me,' Jack Roberts said. 'So perhaps you'll understand that there would be no sense in your struggling — nor in refusing to tell me what I need to know.' Fiercely, he spun her round to face him. 'Where is Saunders then?' he demanded. 'You only need tell me and you'll go free.'

She saw that a filthy sling kept one arm immobilized, and he scowled as he followed her gaze.

'It's no thanks to you that I have not lost the arm; as it is, it's useless still and the surgeon says it'll take weeks to mend. There's nothing I owe you but retribution.'

'What makes you think Mr Saunders had business in Florence?'

'That red-headed beauty in Innsbruck said as much in my hearing. How else would we have known you'd use the Brenner Pass?'

'I don't know where he is and I'd never tell you even if I did know.'

'Fine words, miss,' Roberts scoffed, 'but ones you'll be pleased to retract.'

'I'll tell you nothing.'

'We shall see. I'm not alone, you know; when Taylor did not return I sent for a replacement. Bernard's a fine fellow — six-foot-four he stands and shoulders on him like an ox.'

Georgina turned from Roberts, twisting to free herself. She sensed his surprise, with the one arm alone he was incapable of re-gaining his hold on her. She darted away over the cobbles.

She had not reckoned with the brute's su-perior strength. He was on her before she'd left the inn's archway, his whole weight thrust at her shoulders from behind, drag-ging her down.

'You don't stand a chance, lady,' he sneered. 'And it's time you learned a lesson . . .'

He hauled her to her feet, his hand tearing into her shoulder. 'This way . . .'

Pushing her ahead of him, he was hurry-ing towards a door in one of the outbuild-ings. As they approached, Georgina saw that it gave on to a stable.

The smell of horse was so strong that she retched as he shoved her though the door-way. Roberts was glancing about the gloomy interior. He began propelling her towards a ladder that stood to one end of the stable.

'Since you'll not lead me to Saunders, I must assert some pressure,' he threatened, forcing her ahead of him up the wooden rungs.

Tripping on the hem of her skirt, Georgina stumbled from the ladder into the straw that covered the floor of a loft. There was little opportunity for escape here, with no window and its only access the ladder. And she would have to take care, this upper floor did not cover the entire area of the stable but ended abruptly halfway out from the wall, with a sheer drop to the flagged ground. She felt at her wits' end.

Roberts forced her into the far corner of the wall, thrusting with that strong hand upon her shoulder until she was squatting, her back into the angle, her feet slithering beneath her in shifting straw.

He cackled. 'Where's your dignity now, eh? Are you thinking perhaps to be saying where Saunders is hid? You'll not leave this place till you've told me.'

Georgina said nothing. Roberts was so close that she smelled his sweat along with the stench of horse. His face was only an inch from her own, she caught the reek of garlic, and stale wine.

She flung him from her, startling him so that he lost balance and hurtled towards the edge of the loft as she scrambled to her feet. For one awful moment her relief mingled with dread that she might have sent him to his death, but then he stopped staggering backwards and paused, legs astride, rocking on his heels as he gazed at her.

'Oh, I enjoy a fight,' he declared.

Georgina did not linger. She was stumbling through rustling straw to reach the ladder and stagger down it. Roberts came thudding after her, shaking the rungs beneath her soles.

'Going?' he enquired, scathingly. 'I think not. You've not told me yet where Saunders hides.'

'I have told you, I do not know.' He was almost on top of her as she reached the ground. He snatched at her sleeve but his fingers slipped from the silk and he cursed as Georgina scurried for the door. She fled across the courtyard and darted through its arch. And then she heard shouting; 'Quick, Bernard, seize the wench . . .'

Heavy footfalls followed her, and a hasty glance over her shoulder revealed a man who seemed tall as a giant when he emerged from the inn's yard.

Stumbling between passing carriages, Georgina crossed the road and hurtled down a narrow street that led towards the cathedral. She could hear running footsteps following still but dared not spare time for looking back. Tall, Bernard would possess long legs as well, it would be but a matter of time before he caught her. She must find somewhere to hide — somewhere where he would not dare to seize her.

She half-turned towards the door of the

cathedral but could recall no hiding place within its vast interior. She ran on and she thought of the Uffizi gallery. There, she could take cover and if she located the curator who'd befriended her she would perhaps persuade him to help.

'Georgina!'

In her headlong flight she had not seen Vicenzo striding hurriedly towards her. He looked agitated, and she could not understand why he seemed reluctant to acknowledge her, but she supposed she must present a shocking sight, dishevelled as well as flushed from running.

'Where are you going?' he demanded.

'To — to the Uffizi,' she stammered, glancing back now to see if the huge Bernard was following.

'The gallery is not yet open,' the Conte told her, taking her arm. 'Come, my carriage is just around the corner.'

Sudden relief drained most of the remaining strength from her legs so that Vicenzo was obliged to almost carry her. Once he had settled her against the cushions, he gave her a searching look.

'And from whom were you running?'

Georgina did not answer immediately. She had no intention of telling Il Conte of her determination to quit Florence, nor that

Howard's enemies had reached the city.

'I must have become lost. I found myself in the courtyard of an inn.'

'A most unsuitable place for an unescorted lady.'

'So I learned.'

'I wonder that Howard condones your walking alone in Florence.'

'I doubt that he cares, he's too busy trotting after his wealthy cousin!'

'But . . .' Vicenzo, began, his expression puzzled, but then he smiled. 'It is fortunate then that I was abroad at this ridiculous hour. You have not explained though why you were hastening as though the devil himself was in pursuit.'

'I had been attacked.'

'You mean robbed?'

'No,' she said hastily, 'nothing was taken.'

The Conte was solicitous throughout the journey, then escorted her to her room at the castle before finding Signora Polidori to send a maid to attend Georgina.

When she saw her possessions packing in readiness for leaving, Georgina realized in a flash that she could not go away from Florence until she had seen Howard. She must wait for his return. No one else knew that Roberts and his new accomplice had arrived here, who but she could warn him?

Conte Vicenzo's housekeeper herself brought hot water and towels to Georgina's room and tended her.

'You have had a nasty fright, child, anyone can see that. A little cosseting you shall have.'

Georgina allowed herself to be pampered throughout that day, taking luncheon in her room and only emerging in the evening to dine with her host. He cautioned her to remain indoors on the following day also. Georgina was prepared to do so until Howard arrived.

When she had warned him about Roberts she'd be free to go. She planned every detail of her departure during the enforced retirement in her room, deciding that she would leave, if need be, in darkness. She would find out where the coach called in the city besides the inn where Roberts was staying, and she would make her reservation.

Il Conte seemed concerned about her that evening, glancing frequently towards her during their meal. He was enquiring if she felt up to sitting in the drawing-room when voices were heard in the great hall. Georgina immediately recognized Howard's voice along with Crispino's.

She could wait no longer. Quelling the excitement that surged within her each time that she saw his handsome features, she crossed the hall to his side.

His smile was wide, the blue eyes warming swiftly. 'You could not wait for my company, is that it, my dearest?'

Ignoring the endearment, she steeled herself to speak, only of the threat to him.

'No, I am not so susceptible. Your enemies are here in Florence. I have seen Jack Roberts and an accomplice. They tried to make me reveal where you were. I told them I did not know, but they'll likely seek you out for they did not believe me.'

'Did they harm you?' he asked quickly, his eyes darkening.

She shook her head, biting her lip, not looking at him now lest his magnetism weaken her resolve. 'I do not know what it is that you have done,' she said. 'But I would have no part in your being taken prisoner.'

'I hope that is so,' he remarked lightly, as though choosing to disregard her awkwardness. 'For I intend that you and I will long be held by one bond alone — that which holds man and woman faithful to each other. There'll be neither time nor place for interception by any other . . .'

'Do not jest. I have told you of the danger, that is all.'

'Georgina . . .'

She shrugged off the hand that would have held her while he questioned her formality towards him. And then she was past his side; running up the stairs for all the world as though she feared him.

'Georgina . . .' he repeated. But she forced herself to stare at each stair ahead of her. There could be no looking back to Howard, as there must be no reflection upon the kind of life which they might have had together. He had chosen to go to his cousin and there the matter ended.

Howard frowned. He had returned from Venice with all possible haste, travelling through the night and stopping to eat only as he neared Florence. Exhausted, he felt incapable of reasoning with Georgina. Tomorrow, though, he would take all the time he needed to convince her that she must remain with him always as his wife.

CHAPTER SIXTEEN

Somewhere in the city a clock chimed four of the morning as Georgina stole out of the castle. Still dark, it was far cooler than any night she'd known since her arrival in Florence. Hurrying through the blackness she experienced the dreadful ache that had been with her through the hours that she had lain on her bed. How could she pretend that she did not care that she was leaving Howard when all the while she seemed unable to think of anything but the disillusion she had read in his eyes the previous evening? But it is his own fault, she reminded herself. He should have understood her distress that he had turned to that woman.

Here in the city she was frightened by being alone. Figures huddled in doorways, stirring as she passed, and one man staggered from a doorstep, knocking into her. He reeked of wine and when he pushed his face towards her own Georgina recoiled and darted from him down a side street. She heard footsteps then, following her; glancing back, she saw a young man hurrying to catch up with her. She felt certain he must think her one of the city's easy women to be abroad at this hour. Running on, her belongings an unheeded weight on her arms, she began to out-distance him. But a sudden giddiness made her lean against the wall of a simple roadside dwelling.

She jumped when someone touched her arm. An old woman, darkly clad, questioned her in Italian but Georgina was past being able to speak. She shook her head, freeing herself of the gnarled hand resting on her arm before she stumbled on once more.

She came to a cheap coffee house where the unkempt proprietor was taking down the shutters. Utterly wearied, she took no account of the meagre surroundings and sat at a crude wooden table. She managed to make them understand her request for bread and a hot drink, but she could not tell whether the beverage was chocolate or coffee. And its identity was of total indifference to her.

The urge to leave Florence had deserted her. Since leaving the castle, indeed, all incentive to do anything had disappeared. Without prospect of seeing Howard again, her life had become a grey, haphazard existence. It was of no consequence that she had failed to locate a coaching inn other than the one where she had met Jack Roberts, the idea of returning to her home in Kent was of no more interest than remaining where she was.

'You are English, yes?'

Being addressed in her own tongue startled Georgina into giving the woman pausing at her table a cursory glance.

'That is correct. Why?'

The woman chuckled, though not unkindly. 'You are the first of your kind we've had 'neath our roof. You've lost your way, have you, from the other side of the Arno, in the city?'

'No, I . . . no.'

'But you must be staying in more fashionable parts . . .'

'I am staying nowhere.'

'Now just a minute, miss — you're only a bit of a girl still. It's not wise that you should wander these streets on your own.'

'That is my business,' Georgina stated sharply.

The woman laughed again. 'And that's telling me to mind my own! But I had a daughter once, about your age she'd have been, had she lived. A fine girl, with an English governess, that is how I learned your language.'

'Really?'

'You do not care, do you, not about any-one. What happened, eh?'

Draining her cup ready for leaving, Georgina said nothing.

'We had a grand mansion, my first husband and I, until Bonaparte's men overran it. My man was killed, and all because he tried to keep our home.' She gestured with her head towards the man who was giving orders to a couple of lackeys. 'Giorgio is a good man, he has given me a new name and this place is home now.'

'You are lucky,' Georgina said flatly.

'But you'd have none of this, would you? Too fine you are for the likes of this place.'

'Have I said that?'

'No.' The woman's grey eyes were regarding her keenly. 'If you should be wanting a bed, we could oblige. I'd see any gentlemen were kept from your room to-night.'

For the first time Georgina felt a slight flicker of interest. Too wearied to contemplate travelling away from Florence today, she could not be troubled with seeking a bed.

'Very well then, thank you. I shall be pleased to take a room here.'

The quiet run-down hiding place was just the kind for letting life drift by. No one intruded on her grief. The woman, although amiable, seemed so indefinable that Georgina could have described her to no one. And as for her name, twice Georgina had enquired what it was, and twice had forgotten.

For three entire days she sat in her drab little room, emerging only when called to a meal. The nights seemed long and were un- relieved by sleep but even that fact was a matter of indifference to her.

She felt like one bereaved. Having lost her career and with that the one person whose memory stirred her from lethargy, she ap- peared only half-alive.

'How long are you staying here?' the woman enquired one morning when Georgina was already losing count of the days she had spent there.

'I . . . do not know.'

She noticed the woman's raised eyebrows, and grey eyes searching her face.

Perhaps it was the woman's words, what- ever the reason, Georgina began wondering that night about her reasons for remaining.

'I will leave Florence,' she stated aloud to her room. 'Tomorrow, I will find where the coach departs.'

As soon as she made the resolution she rose, lighting her candle although it wanted half an hour to five in the morning, and gathering together her possessions. She took out her portfolio without thinking of its contents. But as she laid it beside her paints and brushes she felt a twinge of guilt.

These drawings belonged to her husband — commissioned by him, even those remaining unfinished should have been left with Howard. Georgina sighed and began leafing through the sketches, thinking of her distance from the castle. It was impossible to return them to him.

There'll be some means of sending them to him once she'd returned to England, she decided.

The illustration that her subconscious mind had ignored was the one she now held in her hand. And as she saw her watercolour of the beautiful eastern door of the baptistry Georgina gulped, trying to keep back her sobs. But her emotions could be controlled no longer, and as tears poured from her eyes she placed the painting to one side. It seemed to her that she had lost the opportunity not only to finish that particular illustration, but to forge an alliance no less beautiful than those exquisite doors.

'We did work well together,' she assured the humble walls. 'And I would swear my drawings pleased him, if only . . .'

Tired and bemused, she felt incapable of

remembering the reason for her abrupt departure. What was it that could possibly have appeared so important that it sent her away from Howard? Nothing seemed so wrong now as leaving incomplete the finest picture that she might ever accomplish.

She must have slept; daylight awakened her to the fact that she lay on top of crumpled bed covers. A feeble ray of sunlight caught the gleam of gold on her watercolour.

Going to breakfast, Georgina decided to finish the painting before leaving Florence. She would put everything remaining in her into making it a perfect illustration. Perhaps then, receiving it, Howard would recognize that she was by no means entirely untouched by him.

The wan sun lasted less than two hours that day, dark clouds had filled the sky as far as she could see before she had walked to the baptistry. She set up her stool, nevertheless, and took out brushes and her box of colours.

Beginning again on the illustration aroused emotions for which Georgina was unprepared. With each stroke of the brush she recalled some word Howard had used introducing her to the place, a touch of his hand; and more than that, for sitting here

291

resurrected all the happiness that she had felt working with him. And the joy when he'd joined her unexpectedly. If only it were possible to turn back the days to that meeting.

But half an hour into the task and she was compelled to pause, tears obliterated her vision and threatened to spill over and mar the painting. She found a handkerchief and wiped her cheeks then forced herself to continue.

It is only a picture, she asserted silently, finish it and you can go . . .

She bent her head over her work, forcing herself to concentrate despite her longing to be done with it and run away. And when she sensed that she was observed, she resolved to look nowhere but towards her work. She'd spare herself the curious gaze of strangers.

'I hoped that some of your unfinished affairs might claim your attention — eventually.'

The familiar tone made her turn on her stool. Howard's blue eyes were unsmiling and his features appeared stiff as he stood looking down at her. Her eyes blurred then and although she swallowed she could not discipline her emotions.

'You cannot even see the thing,' he exclaimed. 'Come . . .'

Going down on one knee, he collected together her painting equipment and, taking the watercolour from her shaking fingers, helped her to her feet.

'Do not forget your stool,' he said. He might have been a parent leading his little girl away from some source of unhappiness.

Conte Vicenzo's carriage was standing beside the Duomo; silently, Howard assisted her inside. She heard him instructing the coachman then felt the jogging motion as they drove away.

When her tears began to clear and she gazed through the window they were some distance into the hills, the city was out of sight. Howard called the man to halt, and then he faced her.

'Well?' he demanded.

'I know it was wrong of me to take the drawings, they were yours. I understand that now, I thought of them in the night, and would have returned them to you.'

He snorted. 'Indeed? Do you suppose I *cared*, about them.'

'But your book,' she interrupted, 'you need illustrations.'

'*That!*' he exclaimed violently, 'do you think that matters!'

'You mean . . .'

'Georgina . . .' He took both her hands in his while the strong eyes seemed to haul her towards him. He scanned her face as though to plough through to her soul. 'For days and nights I have wrestled with my conscience to find ought that I might have done to make you run from me.'

'But . . .'

'I didn't know where to look. My only hope was that you would return to finish your picture of the baptistry doors.' The faintest of smiles hovered at his lips. 'You were an intolerable time over deciding to do so.'

'You mean . . . ?'

'Each day, for as long as daylight lasted, I have waited around the cathedral square.'

'But . . .'

He stared down at the hands still clinging to her slender fingers. 'We need speak no more of that, sufficient that my vigil succeeded.'

'But why, Howard, why? When all the time you are so bewitched by your cousin that you could not keep from her?'

'When I am *what?*' he roared.

'You cannot have the both of us. I'll share you with no woman.'

'Who said ought of sharing? When you really are mine there'll scarce be time for work, much less for any other person!'

'You cannot deny that you sought her in Venice.'

'And you, had you listened, might have learned the reason. You're over fond of leaping to conclusions and judgements, Georgina, when you know nothing of the circumstances.'

'I knew enough.'

'Is that so? You were aware, were you, that I met with Lady Virginia to settle an old debt. So that I'd be free of her. That I made it plain we'd meet but the once again, when I remove my belongings from the home to which her father once welcomed me — and in which my own poverty compelled that I remain.'

'Howard, don't . . .'

'You'll hear me out now I've begun. You'll misjudge me no longer! I have worked for years to discharge the debt to Virginia's family, because that — and that alone — tethered me to her. You should have known that with *our* first meeting mastery over my own future became imperative. You are my wife, Georgina, and I'll shift the earth itself to have you live as such!'

'Oh, Howard, I was so afraid I'd lost you.'

He crushed her to him, his lips finding hers. When her teeth parted for his tongue she felt his hands bruising her shoulders as if willing her to merge with him.

'I'm taking you to the castle, or I swear I'll have you, here in this carriage! There's but a hair's breadth holds me from teaching you where you belong.'

Again his lips claimed hers while he held her so close that it seemed their very nerve endings combined, producing a tingling that made clothing immaterial. His breath was swift against her cheek, then stirring her hair, and she felt her own quick response, a sighing interrupted only by her urgent kisses.

His hand cupped her breast now, the satin of her gown gliding between his skin and her own, exciting her until she felt she could not bear that his touch should ever quit her. Her fingers traced his lean thigh, caressing, seeking, and feeling the tremor that acknowledged her, while her whole being seemed to pulse in tune with his.

'You're mine now,' he told her, 'you are truly mine.'

They drove in the Conte's *cabriolet* to collect her belongings from the drab lodging. And then it was home with Howard to his friend's *castello,* and even the rain lashing upon the carriage could not mute their high spirits. They ran through the rivulets rushing down the hillside to swirl about the court-yard and laughing, hand-in-hand, hurried up the steps to toll the bell for admittance.

Signora Polidori opened to them, muttering that the man-servant, Crispino, had gone to his home. She appeared not only surprised to see Georgina, but perturbed.

'A moment,' she said, detaining them in the hall. 'I must speak with Il Conte.'

She crossed swiftly to the dining-room, closing its heavy door after her. She emerged after a brief few seconds, her face unsmiling.

'Il Conte would speak with you, if you please, sir,' she stated rather stiffly to Howard.

When Georgina made to accompany him, Signora Polidori barred her way. 'No, not you, signorina, the Conte wishes to speak with Signor Saunders alone.'

Vicenzo rose and beckoned Howard further into the room. He watched until his housekeeper had shut the door, then began speaking without inviting his friend to sit.

'The news I have is serious — I would that you had not brought Miss Morton to us now.'

Howard frowned. 'But I do not understand. You know how I have searched the whole of Florence these past few days. You said nothing then of your reluctance to have her here.'

'Because then I knew nothing of certain matters which now make it quite impossible that she remain.'

'What can you mean? I must ask that you speak more plainly.'

'As you will. You have heard, I believe, of the theft at the Uffizi.'

'It was *I* who told you of the uniformed men surging around the place, after they'd discovered the forgery of the Leonardo drawing.'

'Quite.'

'But what is that to do with . . .' Howard glanced to Vicenzo's scowling face. 'Oh, no. Oh God, no!'

'The authorities were here less than an hour ago. They brought an ancient curator from the Uffizi. He led them here. It seems he was familiar with the girl already when he saw her one day copying the Leonardo.'

'This cannot be. She would not.'

'I fear, my friend, there can be no other conclusion. The old man recognized my *cabriolet,* which he had seen Georgina using. You are as aware as I of her skill, you cannot deny that she would be capable of such a reproduction.'

'But I do deny that she would attempt

anything of the kind.'

'Your defence of her does you credit, would that it were less misplaced. You have taken the news badly, as I feared you would, you have my sympathy although you will understand that I cannot keep the girl under my roof. She slipped from here, you know, early on the morning of the theft. I saw her myself later, near the Uffizi.'

'But Georgina has the highest of standards. You know that!'

The Conte shrugged.

'A sad trait — that one wishes in others an honesty one is not prepared to practise.'

'How dare you!'

'I dare, my dear Howard, because I am not so besotted with the girl as to overlook evidence. You believe now that she must be innocent, soon you will see how misguided you've been in supposing her so. Meanwhile, if you'd ask her to step inside I will speak with her.'

'No. No. She has nowhere to go, she . . .'

'I imagine that the authorities will have somewhere in mind for her.'

'A stinking gaol! Are you insane that you'd condemn her to that!'

'She has condemned herself. And I fear that you are the one devoid of sense!'

'Vicenzo, think what you are doing! You

cannot let her be imprisoned.'

Il Conte smiled, though his dark eyes remained pitiless. 'Oh, I can. It is the duty of every citizen to uphold justice.'

'I'll be hanged if I'll let you turn the girl from here!'

'Take care, my friend, or *hanged* is what you'll be as her accomplice.'

'And you'd have her convicted, wouldn't you, allowing no opportunity for proving her innocence.'

'What choice have I?'

'Give Georgina shelter here while she prepares her defence. I'll swear that she had no part in this.'

'I'll not have my family name implicated in this sordid business.'

'At least let me talk with her, give us some time before you drive us out.'

'My dear Howard, I am not withdrawing my hospitality from yourself.'

'I'll not stay, unless Georgina remains with me.'

'As you wish.' Il Conte turned his back. As Howard reached the door, however, he called him back. 'There was one additional matter . . .'

'Yes?' A hand on the handle, Howard spoke wearily, without turning.

'Whilst the authorities were here they

raised the subject of your travelling into the Tuscan hills.'

'Oh?' Frowning again, Howard faced the Conte. 'What is this?'

'Certain documents happened to come into their possession.'

'Documents? Do you mean my maps? How on earth did they lay their hands on those?'

Vicenzo shrugged. 'They insisted, quite naturally, on searching my home for evidence of Miss Morton's cunning. It was unfortunate that they had learned also of your supposed treachery.'

Howard glared at the Conte then stormed from the room. 'If those maps have gone,' he shouted over his shoulder, 'I'll hold you responsible!'

'They said they would return,' Vicenzo called after him. 'I believe they would question you.'

Georgina sped to Howard's side and placed a hand on his arm.

'What is it?' she demanded.

'Nothing,' he replied. 'Nothing.'

'There must be something,' she persisted, running beside him as he scaled the stairs two at a time. At the door of his room he fumbled with the handle, but then he was striding to a drawer in the tall chest. Refusing even to contemplate the accusation against Georgina, he was concentrating on a charge that seemed less menacing.

In his urgency he tore the drawer from its runner, scattering its contents on the carpet. He dropped to his knees, gathering up papers and scanning each one anxiously.

'Oh, Lord . . . Oh, Lord!'

'Howard . . .' Kneeling at his side, Georgina tried to make him look at her, but it was only after considerable effort that she gained his attention.

'The maps, the maps,' he murmured. 'What in hell's name can I do?'

'Someone's taken them, is that it?'

He nodded. '*Someone* being the authorities — magistrates, or whatever their equivalent here. They'll have me gaoled. And then where's the opportunity for proving my innocence? How will I tell them my true purpose and have them believe me?'

'Howard, I am sorry,' she began quietly. 'But if you'd been more honest about your task . . .'

'Honest?' he shouted, staring at her as though he hardly recognized her face. 'Honest? You're a fine one, aren't you, to tax me with being less than honest!'

'What do you mean?' She sprang to her feet and he stood also, facing her, his expression stern.

'You left early from this place, did you not? Not only on the morning that you finally left the castle but also on the previous day?'

'I did, yes. Of what consequence is that?'

He paused before speaking again. 'Georgina — will you tell me your reasons for going out so secretly?'

Remembering how she had intended leaving Florence because she had believed Howard gone eagerly to his cousin, she felt this was entirely the wrong moment for voicing her doubts, and said nothing.

Her silence seemed eloquent of her guilt. Howard groaned. 'I understand.'

'You do not. And I haven't the slightest notion what you mean.'

'No? You'll tell me next you've never seen the forgery that now hangs in place of Leonardo's drawing at the Uffizi gallery.'

'Leonardo da Vinci?' she gasped. *'Drawing?'*

'So, it is not unknown to you.' He turned from her.

Georgina's fingers flew to her face as she tried to still her sudden trembling. The Leonardo drawing . . . ! How or why she couldn't understand, but evidently she'd been tricked into assisting in a reckless theft. But how could Howard's friend, Vicenzo, contrive to have her appear guilty?

303

Unless . . . unless . . .

Again, Howard sighed. 'Vicenzo claims the authorities have sought you here, and will return. Go to your room and wait there till I come for you. I am going into the city where I'll do all I can to set this matter to rights. Give me the original and I'll return it to . . .'

'The original? You cannot — *cannot* believe I would attempt any such thing? Vicenzo had me make that copy — I sold it to him.'

Howard lowered his troubled gaze, then spoke slowly, 'At first, I would have none of Il Conte's tale, but then . . . you must admit it did correspond with your behaviour. And Vicenzo claims you appeared distraught when he saw you near the Uffizi . . .'

'Of course I was — I had just escaped from that evil man Roberts.'

'True, you did caution me afterwards . . .' Howard hesitated, longing to accept her word. 'But why didn't you tell me just now why you went out so early?'

Georgina sighed. 'Do you never seek to conceal some motive that might hurt another, especially when that person is someone you love? Are *you* always so scrupulously truthful when I question you?'

'Go on . . .'

Somewhere below them Vicenzo was shouting at the servants and doors were slamming, but to her nothing existed beyond this room and the man whose eyes challenged hers.

She swallowed. 'I went to a coaching inn to reserve a seat on the northbound mail. I could not . . . *felt* that I could not stay with you when I feared you loved Lady Virginia.'

'Georgina! A fine mess we've made . . .'

She nodded. 'But that's in the past. We should be thinking now of how to set things right.'

'Would that it were so simple.'

'Wouldn't your friend in England, in these circumstances, reveal his reasons for commissioning you?'

'Perhaps.'

'But what is it that makes your maps appear so sinister?'

'Did I not tell you — they are extremely detailed, and show routes from each area to a major port.'

'Oh. But who could be interested in such information?'

'A merchant who is planning to establish himself in the growing wine trade.'

'Is that all? But how . . . ?'

'Paul Hardaker is an old friend. When he learned of my travels he suggested I might find out more about vineyards in which he has an interest. And so, first in Portugal and now here, I have prepared records of those vineyards which should yield good harvests.'

'But if it were that innocent why couldn't you have told those who accused you of spying?'

'And have every interested party bidding in those areas where Paul would invest?'

'And now — now that you are at such grave risk?'

'I shall explain, and trust that I am believed. And I shall send to York, begging Paul to substantiate my word.'

'But that could take too long . . .'

Howard's face was grim. 'I know. I have to face the probability of being gaoled to await such proof.'

'Oh, Howard, take care — do nothing to make the authorities unsympathetic . . .'

Georgina walked with him down the staircase and through the great hall. When he opened the door rain was falling like some stiffened veil.

'You cannot go out in this,' she protested. 'I'll go to the Uffizi gallery and tell them the truth.'

'I must. I'll make them listen.' Howard pulled up the collar of his coat. 'I'll find

Vicenzo's coachman and ask him to drive me into the city. Keep away from Vicenzo while I'm absent and maybe he'll think that we have left together.'

'Howard . . .'

He drew her to him for a lingering kiss.

'You'd best close this door, the floor is awash already. And for God's sake keep to your room. The upper floors should be safe from flooding.'

After watching him run down the steps to the driveway, Georgina did as he'd told her. The entire courtyard was already covered with several inches of water and it was beginning to lap over the steps leading to the door.

But how could she worry that Howard must be abroad in such dreadful weather when her heart was leaden, not on account of her own predicament but of his.

CHAPTER SEVENTEEN

Although she knew that Howard had gone to try and prove her innocence, Georgina became terrified that she would be taken prisoner before his return. She had seen how torn he was between remaining here with her and going to the gallery. She was in danger, she knew, not only of arrest but from the flooding. If only there was something she might do, something to support her own explanation about the drawing.

Glancing to the door of the dining-room which remained closed, she crept silently towards the foot of the staircase. Her slippered feet noiseless upon the carpet, she ran up to the first landing. There, she hurried past her own room and on towards the back stair that she knew.

She sped upwards and along corridors over the remembered route to the studio door. And when she stood with heart thudding while she reached for its handle she found the room unlocked. With a sigh of relief, she slipped inside.

The studio was lighter than the rest of the

castle which had darkened with the storm, but the ferocity of the rain lashing against the huge panes of glass was quite frightening. Just for a moment she stared over the swift-flowing Arno and the city, and blinked when lightning dazzled her. The thunder that cracked seconds later made her start, but seemed to stress the need for haste.

Looking about her, Georgina noticed canvases stacked against the walls, with others, incomplete, lying about on tables and on an oak chest as if laid out for drying. One canvas stood on an easel with Vicenzo's palette to one side and on a second easel another painting, apparently identical with the one on which he worked, the only difference being that this canvas was completed whereas the other . . .'

'He *is* making copies,' she murmured, her suspicions now confirmed. 'He must be substituting them for the originals and . . .' Mid-sentence, she ceased all conjecture. Vicenzo's occupation was not her concern. But she must find the Leonardo stolen from the Uffizi.

Georgina darted about the room, ferreting through first one stack of pictures, then another, and a third, but she failed to find the drawing. She went to the tables, each had a drawer, but each drawer produced nothing.

She went swiftly to the oak chest and, carefully, set aside the paintings. She raised the carved lid and gazed down into a confusion of documents. In such a place one might conceal a drawing . . .

Absorbed in her search, conscious only of rain beating upon the window, she heard nothing when the door behind her opened and a soft tread crossed the studio.

A hand clawed at her shoulder and she was hauled to her feet, then swung round with her back against the wall.

'It had to be you, meddling with my possessions,' Vicenzo snarled.

He slammed down the lid of the chest, splitting the fine carving.

'I need not enquire what you seek, but you'll not find the masterpiece here.'

'You admit to handling it then.'

'I admit nothing — and neither you nor any other will prove a thing against me. Yours was the work, and yours will be the punishment.'

Her gaze strayed involuntarily to the easel and to its twin holding the painting he was copying.

Il Conte laughed. 'You have only today realized, have you not? And I feared you had guessed my purpose from the first. I could have saved myself anxiety. But no matter, my secret now is safe.'

Georgina knew he intended she would never leave his home. Her heart had pounded when he entered, surprising her, now it seemed about to burst from her breast in frenzy. But she'd not permit him to recognize her fright, nor would she let it paralyze her.

'You cannot keep me here,' she stated, marvelling at her own calm voice.

'No? And who will prevent me?'

'I need only scream . . .'

'And who is there to hear you? Saunders is gone, the servants also — terrified by the swelling of the Arno.'

Aghast, she stared at him.

He was edging backwards; casting a hasty glimpse over his shoulder, he reached for a palette knife. And then he continued, his gaze steady upon her, 'You also should have left. As it is, you give me no alternative.'

Slowly, he was advancing, the knife poised.

Georgina ducked, and swivelled on her low heels, to run the length of the studio, but before she reached the door she heard the Conte's swift breath behind her. He grasped her arm, turning her to face him while he pressed the knife at her throat.

'You can run nowhere that I may not

311

reach. Go tearing through the entire *castello* and you do but waste your effort for I will surely kill you.'

'I shall live,' she shouted back, dark eyes glinting, 'if only to declare you a forger and see you charged! I shall clear my name.'

'You will do nothing, nothing!'

She kicked out at his shins and he flinched, but his grip upon her did not relax, and the knife still probed at her throat. She kicked again, thankful that her father had taught her to fight like a boy. She stamped on his foot and his fingers eased on her arm. Swiftly, she writhed free of him and felt behind her for the door handle. He lunged for her but she kicked a third time, wildly, and read pain in his face.

The door opened. Risking a knife in her back, Georgina spun from him and bolted. On the steps, she paused. Far below her in the well of the stair, water swirled. The castle was flooded.

Turning quickly, Georgina ran up the spiral stair, praying that she'd not miss her footing for here it was almost black as night. Il Conte hurtled after, so close upon her heels that fear prickled the length of her spine and raised the hair to the back of her head.

Higher and higher, she climbed, grazing a

hand on the wall, skinning her shin against a step.

Even above the howling of the wind, she heard his heavy breathing which drove her on, against the protest of her own labouring heart and aching lungs.

The chase was like a nightmare, her pulsing head incapable of thought, her trembling legs staggering on, yet seeming to make no progress, until she imagined her climb could cease only in her own collapse.

And then she was beside a door, pushing hard against some strength that seemed to press from its other side.

The gale battered rain into her face, stinging tears to her eyes, and drenching the hair that flapped about her head. In a moment her gown was saturated to cling icily in the wind. And then Vicenzo was there, laughing above the storm.

'You have trapped yourself,' he scoffed, his eyes black and gleaming. He shoved her roughly against the turreted wall surrounding the tower.

'See!' he yelled, forcing her to gaze down to the torrent that had been the peacefully flowing Arno. 'There's no escape from here.'

Georgina reeled, dizzily, wondering if she'd fall and save him the task of killing her.

He pinioned her against the wall with his body, imprisoning her hands in one of his own. The knife's blade shone as it neared her throat again.

Georgina stiffened, her breathing suspended, as she waited for the thrust that would end her life. She was kicking at Vicenzo again, but no more effectively than a feather might trouble iron.

I cannot die, something inside her screamed. I cannot lose the chance of going on, working with Howard, loving him. I cannot die . . .

The raging of the storm was inside her head, a thundering of pulses, until she and the elements seemed fused. The sudden rumbling that shook the campanile might have been the fracturing of her skull. Yet somehow she sensed its source was beyond her. Her hands were freed.

Vicenzo's gaze slid to the sodden landscape below. Glancing to every side, in a frenzy, Georgina saw a stout rope and hauled on it. A bell tolled discordantly, vibrating the tower. Both she and Vicenzo started.

He sprang from her. In two strides he had gained the door and was through it to the stair. She reached the door as he bolted it, locking her out on the summit of the tower.

She rested against one wall, sobbing out great gasps of relief. Prisoner she might be, but she was alive. Anxiously wondering what had perturbed Vicenzo, she leaned cautiously over the battlement.

The Arno had burst its banks. Just upstream of the castle a screen of water was obliterating the Conte's gardens, swirling to cover trees and surging up the walls towards the ground floor windows. Had she not known of Vicenzo's presence she would have believed now that nothing in the whole world existed beside herself to witness this invasion.

She was still gazing, fascinated, when a tiny boat was pushed out from the side of the *castello* beyond her line of vision. She saw Vicenzo taking up its oars, and what appeared to be a heap of pictures in the bows.

He glanced upwards, and though she could not see his expression clearly she sensed that it would be evil.

'You're my prisoner still,' he shouted. 'By morning when the floods subside I'll have brought those who'll arrest you . . .' His cries were carried away by the wind until she could no longer see the tossing boat.

With Vicenzo gone, Georgina felt calmer. She looked round her immediate surroundings. Again, she went to the door but it remained unyielding.

Here, on top of the campanile, rain water was swishing about her ankles. Chilled already by soaking garments, her legs and feet developed intense cramp which no amount of walking back and forth could relieve.

'I'll not stay out here all night,' she asserted to the wind, and felt better immediately. And there was only one means of leaving the tower. She leaned over its parapet again. Some way below and to her right was a window, only small, but wider than the slit next to the door here. Somehow, she must reach that window.

Peering through the gloom, pausing to draw wet strands of hair away from her eyes, she carefully examined the wall.

There were footholds, stones protruding beyond their neighbours: employing extreme care, she might reach the window and find refuge.

Anything, Georgina knew, was preferable to waiting helplessly for Vicenzo's return. She tugged the bell-rope free and, securing it to a battlement, was grateful for its support. Fighting giddiness, she scrambled up on to the wall and, gingerly, lowered one foot into space behind her.

Rain and wind lashed at her skirts so that they clung against her legs then flapped at her side like some weighty penant. God, she thought, I cannot do this!

'I will *not* fall,' she kept telling herself. 'I must not. I would never see Howard again, never put pencil to paper, never . . . never again see anything so lovely as those baptistry doors.'

She swallowed hard then felt around with her toe until she found a protruding stone. Trusting one hand and the rope for support while she launched the other foot into space was terrifying. Yet she dared not turn back.

Carefully stretching out each foot in turn to a tenuous foothold, and clinging to the saturated masonry, she finally reached the window.

Gasping in agitation, she hung on to the rope while she steeled herself to thrust the other fist through the glass. At her second attempt the window fell inwards to tinkle in fragments on to the floor.

Careless of scratches, she eased herself through the splinters still clinging to the frame. Exhausted, close to hysteria, she lay where she had landed until her breathing steadied.

Presently, somewhat recovered, Georgina stumbled to her feet; treading carefully through the broken glass, she found her way towards the familiar spiral stair. With a glance down to the water that seemed to have risen frighteningly high, she began slowly to descend. Soon she was running along corridors until, at last, she reached her own room.

Slowly, she gazed about its shabby interior, thinking how she had supposed never to see again this welcome drabness. Rushing to the window, she saw that the water outside was only three feet beneath her balcony, and she prayed it would rise no higher.

Georgina went swiftly to light her candle and stripped off her sodden clothing. She found a towel to rub herself dry. Thrusting on a clean chemise, she staggered across to lie weakly on the bed.

She rested there, unable to force strength into her quivering legs. Thunder came and went, shattering the skies over the city, echoing from its hills, and shaking the castle to its water-logged foundations. When the lightning split black clouds it seemed to slither over the water to menace her. And though she had long since ceased to watch the steady advance of the torrent climbing the wall, nothing could block its lapping from her ears.

If only she were not alone, if only Howard were here. For then she might have endured this waiting which, she feared, would end in drowning. With him she'd not have been swept into this terror, which seemed bordering on madness.

Nothing appeared natural this night, nothing normal. Each noise carried by the restless gale beyond her window seemed eerie as a cemetery. And now the lapping water had a different tone, as though some evil sprite were struggling through to seize her. It came nearer and nearer, until she longed for this weird inexorable being to end her solitary fear.

The sound stilled, giving way to a loud panting and groaning progressing up the wall beneath her window. Some heavy object came slurring over the balustrade, thudding on to her balcony. There was a slap, slap as if the Arno itself had taken feet and was walking to her window. Georgina stiffened; it could be Vicenzo . . .

A rapping on the glass startled a scream from her which evoked a strange, breathy laughter from outside in the darkness.

'Georgina . . .'

She was out of the bed and across by the window as swiftly as a bird as she recognized the voice. He was naked from the waist upwards and drenched, but with no heed for her chemise she flung her arms about him.

'Howard! Oh, thank God! Oh, Howard.'

His kiss filled her whole being, but then

he tried to move away.

'These breeches have shrunk with immersion so that they threaten to ruin me. I must go and . . .'

'You will go nowhere, not even to the next room. I have waited here alone, terrified, praying for your safe return. Do you think I'll have us separated now for any purpose?'

'But . . .'

'I am your wife!'

The candle revealed that Howard went now to the fastening of his breeches. 'I wish I could think we'll ever live a married life. The truth is, my love, I could not find any man who'd listen. Those who keep order here are preserving their homes against the flood. But by morning they'll be back on duty. And then we'll both be imprisoned.'

'You should have left for England, and found your friend to exonerate you.'

'And leave you here? No, Georgina. Whate'er transpires I'll not desert you.'

He gathered her to him, kissing her, and receiving from her lips the response he needed.

'But there's work to do, my girl; to prove your innocence we must find that Leonardo drawing.'

'I have searched and can find nothing.'

'We'll search some more, when I am

dressed more decently.'

Going to his room, Howard could not have guessed at her turmoil. She had longed for the reassurance of his company, but now her entire person was stirred by his embrace until she could think only of pressing herself ever closer to his hard body. Desire pulsed through her, but she must dismiss it.

'I'm afraid that the Conte has left, taking the drawing with him,' she said.

'He has done what . . . ?' Howard knotted a towel about his waist as he appeared at his door. Georgina came from her own room.

'He found me searching for the Leonardo and tried to kill me.'

'God, he's marked you — are those his scratches?'

She touched her face and neck. 'No, that was the broken window.'

He frowned, his eyes questioning.

'I found out he'd been forging pictures. I'm certain he was the one who made that substitution. He locked me out on top of the bell tower.'

'And . . . ?'

'I climbed down.'

'How — *climbed?*'

'How do you suppose?'

'Georgina! You could have been killed!'

He came to draw her to him, heedless now

321

of everything except the pain he felt in the mere contemplation of losing her.

'I want you to live,' he cried, pulling her against him, 'with me, always. You're not to risk your life ever again, you must promise me.'

'Yes, Howard.'

His lips were fierce on hers, his hands restless over her body, as he held her close.

'God, that I knew a way to keep us both from prison! It'll tear out my heart, Georgina, to have you taken from me.'

She seemed to see herself imprisoned, separated from this man who had become her whole world, aching to learn what he was enduring.

'If only we'd had a proper wedding,' she whispered, 'there'd be a bond then that nought could sever.'

'I know. I know. For so long now I've been determined to renew those vows I made ...'

'Because you mean them to last?'

'I meant that from the start. But I beg favours of no one. How else could I have asked you to share my danger? How could I have asked you to stay by me when debt prevented my owning a home fit to give my bride?'

For a while he was quiet, standing a pace or so from her though with both hands on her shoulders. And then he cleared his throat.

Gently, he took her right hand, slid the ring from it and, placing it on her left hand, retained her fingers in his grasp. Speaking softly, he sought her gaze, his blue eyes brilliant with emotion.

'I, Howard take thee Georgina, to my wedded wife, to have and to hold from this day forward, for better for worse, for richer for poorer, in sickness and in health, to love and to cherish, till death us do part, according to God's holy ordinance; and thereto I plight thee my troth.'

His kiss sealed his words as his arms drew her to him. And now he permitted his eager self expression of his love. One hand gently cupped her breast, stroking its firm peak, while his other fingers traced the curve of her spine and sensed the tremor beneath his touch. The thin chemise, wet from his own body, slithered against her smooth skin, increasing the enticement. Her lips moved beneath his, and parted, admitting his tongue in token of her welcome of him. Closer than ever before he held her, as though to become her preservation.

Georgina sighed, closing her eyes whilst she thrust her fingers into the thick wet hair curling at his ear, holding his face close upon her own as if with her kisses to absorb him. Her arm was about his body, every nerve alert to the feel of strong moist flesh.

Above the low neck of her chemise the chest crushing against her breasts was warming with their contact yet damp still, so that the slightest movement was pure excitement. And neither was still, for how could she remain so when he was stirring ceaselessly, caressing her entire person. The towel he wore had long since parted and she rejoiced, recognizing his need of her.

A great throbbing, commencing deep within her, seemed to echo the pressure that was upon her from thigh to breasts. She heard a moan and scarcely knew it for her own.

Howard was edging her backwards, slowly, further into the room. But the bed was yards away and before they reached it she felt the silken wall-covering cool to her back, in sharp contrast to the warmth that anchored her there. She felt the towel slither to the carpet and urgent fingers taking her chemise. And now the whole of him clung to her.

Her fingers caressed the line of his hips then down over his thigh before travelling upwards, intimately fondling.

He smiled and now his lips went to the

tantalizing curve of her ivory shoulder, and down over the soft skin to her pert breasts, and though his kisses were urgent, Georgina sensed a new tenderness there. Every touch accelerated her pulsing to mingle with the rapid breath that punctuated kisses when his mouth returned to hers. Quivering, her legs required the bed's support when, gently, he laid her there.

Briefly, he lingered, one arm about her, fingers steadily winning from her such excitement that she longed for fulfilment. Quietly, he smiled and for a time his gaze linked with hers and then he was probing between her thighs. A shiver of delight ran through her and readily she arched to him, thrilling to the thrusting that asserted she was his.

She felt her own body grasping him, drawing him even closer, reflecting each movement that carried him deeper within.

'I love you, Georgina,' he said exultantly, gloriously happy.

CHAPTER EIGHTEEN

Once, in the night, Georgina wakened. Remembering, she smiled and curved into the warmth of the man slumbering beside her. Beyond their window the storm had gusted away its fury, and the surging of the Arno sounded less urgent.

Dawn brought Howard's kisses to tease lips and cheek until she acknowledged him. His smile was half-rueful as he regarded her.

'You ensured last night that all thought of searching for the Leonardo be delayed!'

'Are you regretful then?' she enquired lightly.

He shook his head, the blue eyes deepening. 'Never that, but I'm haunted by the dread of separation. Life teaches sombre lessons.'

'And glorious ones also. In loving . . .'

'You feel no apprehension then?'

'You are here.'

'H'm.'

'I'll not tarnish one minute of your company. Nor waste it. Since we postponed our search for the Leonardo original we'll make good our intent now before any can find their way here.'

After dressing swiftly they went together to Vicenzo's studio. On the threshold, Georgina gasped at the chaos. The reproduction was gone from the Conte's easel, its original likewise vanished. As soon as she began searching she found that many of the paintings there the previous day were missing now. A glance towards the oaken chest revealed its splintered lid open, the contents thrown around as if someone in great haste had sifted them.

'That was the only place I had no opportunity for searching,' she said. 'If that was where he'd concealed the Leonardo drawing it'll be gone.'

They looked, nevertheless, before turning dejectedly from the room.

'I'm certain he had some pictures with him in the boat. If he hadn't disposed already of the da Vinci he wouldn't leave it here.'

Howard nodded. 'I'm sure you are right. We can only hope we somehow reach Vicenzo before he has passed it on.'

Georgina sighed. 'I still do not understand, not completely. Not why he had me make that copy . . .'

'Surely because although he worked

adroitly with paint and brushes he was un-
accomplished at drawing . . .'

'You mean he was determined to replace
the Leonardo with a fake, and then what?
Sell the original?'

'What else? I cannot credit that all the
copies he produced were for a legitimate
market.'

'Certainly he was furious when he supposed I suspected he was involved in some
forgery.'

'Precisely.'

'Oh, Howard, whatever can we do?'

'Follow him!'

They went down the great staircase where
silt clung to the walls. The exquisite carpet
had been rolled, saturated, from the steps.
Crispino was sweeping away water from the
marble flooring. Paddling in the murky
dregs, he somehow retained his customary
dignity.

Crispino half-turned towards them. 'Il
Conte is detained . . .' he began.

'Detained?' Georgina and Howard asked
in unison.

'In hospital. Word arrived as I came here
by boat from my family's home.'

'Il Conte Vicenzo is ill?' Howard enquired
dubiously.

'Injured, alas. They found him concussed,

at the height of the storm. His boat was over-turned; a tree, felled by the gale, trapped him against a boulder.' The man-servant sighed, shaking his head. 'Why could he not have remained here? He had my word I'd return at daybreak.'

Georgina glanced briefly to Howard, then again to Crispino.

'The boat. Was it empty?'

'So I believe. Who can say? Who cares so long as the master is alive.'

'You say you came yourself by boat?' Howard asked.

'*Si, signor.* It was the only way, the road is impassable, most of the grounds here under water still.'

'May I borrow it?'

'You, *signor?* Are you thinking to visit Il Conte?'

'I would be grateful for use of your boat,' Howard asserted.

'Take it and welcome. There's plenty to occupy me here for yet awhile.'

'You wait here, Georgina,' Howard told her as they turned to hurry away.

'I shall not,' she responded quietly. 'Now wc are one I'll bear no separation.'

'Please,' he began, but she was adamant and walked swiftly at his side while he strode through the castle to where the rowing boat was moored at the rear.

'*Are* we going to Vicenzo?' she asked as he assisted her into the bobbing craft.

'Not yet. Since no one else has searched for anything that might have survived the wrecking of his boat it's time we did.'

'You think we might find something?'

He smiled slightly, glancing towards her as he took up the oars. 'Hope exists always,' he said.

Although the level of the Arno had declined tremendously, it flowed fiercely still, rushing them towards first one bank and then the other.

'I'd have been easier had I known you were safe at the castle,' Howard observed, steering the craft as carefully as he could between rocks strewn about by the flooding.

'And I'd be easier if you'd preserve your breath for rowing, rather than chiding me for a matter already decided.'

He laughed, astonishing her. 'Lord, deliver us both from all threat of imprisonment so that I may take time to curb your will!'

Georgina smiled wide-eyed back at him. 'Do you suppose you'd achieve that? When you're the very man who has made me strengthen my will-power!'

'How do you reckon so?'

'You made me prove myself — first as an artist; but then as a woman determined to match a man's endurance in travel.'

'You've not found journeying with me easy then?'

'And if I admit to that — what then?'

He smiled. 'I'll risk inflating your head by praising your spirit! Though I doubt I'll ever again know the peace of a day without your challenging!'

'My . . .' Her voice broke off and then she screamed. 'Howard, take care!'

A tree was almost blocking their passage as, wedged against a boulder, it leaned over the river.

'I suppose this is where Vicenzo came to grief,' Howard said, shipping an oar to free a hand for holding them off from the tree trunk.

As they passed Georgina gazed keenly towards the banks to either side while their boat ran swiftly with the river.

'Any sign of the pictures?' Howard asked.

'None. There is a mass of debris, but nothing resembling paintings.'

'I imagine anything remaining with Vicenzo thus far, would have been swept along for some distance further. The swell was enormous when I swam back last evening, and the current powerful.'

'So we could well have some way still to go?'

He grinned at her. 'Are you enjoying my company the less now? You should not waste the moment nor — what was it — "tarnish one minute". I'll remember that phrase, against the times when you are tiring of me!'

'I'll never do that.'

'Is that your vow? If that were so I'd fetch my pen and have you write such a fine promise!'

'Howard,' she said, suddenly grave, 'let us but survive through these difficulties, and I'll tolerate all manner of things with you.'

'I know,' he said. 'I know. Do you not believe my own sentiments are similar? Let us but endure.' He frowned. 'Pray God we find proof of your innocence.'

Nearing the Ponte Vecchio, they saw that dwellings on the river banks were mud encrusted almost to the level of nearby streets, but there, it appeared, the encroaching waters had checked. All about each support of the bridge refuse was heaped, abandoned by the receding river. Broken timbers from boats once moored at its banks, branches from trees, wheels and other fragments of a carriage swept into the water.

Here, so many rocks had been flung together that it was impossible for their craft to pass beyond the bridge.

'We'd best pull in to the side.'

'No, wait,' Georgina protested. 'Don't you see — if we search here, this is just the spot where any debris would be caught.'

Laboriously, Howard manœuvred their craft around each of the two central supports of the old bridge, fending off with an oar when they drifted in too closely. Georgina leaned from the boat, peering into the assortment of wreckage, willing into existence some evidence of the Leonardo drawing.

'It's no use,' she cried presently, 'if it was ever in the river the drawing must have disintegrated.' Her eyes pricked with unshed tears. 'If you would put in now, beside the Uffizi, I will go inside. I will speak first with the old curator. I fear he'll not believe me, but he will know whom I must see.'

Silently, Howard tied up at the river bank then helped her out on to mud that oozed over their shoes.

'Careful of your step,' he cautioned, but Georgina was heedless now of anything. They had tried to locate the one item that could have cleared her, and they had failed.

No one would believe her. She was unknown here, to be mistrusted, whilst Il Conte Vicenzo wag a highly respected citizen of this city.

'Do not forget,' Howard told her, 'I am

with you, whatever . . .'

Unable to speak, she nodded.

'Georgina, wait . . .'

A pace or so behind, Howard was on his knees, grovelling in the stinking mud. 'Here's a frame or some thing . . .'

Dropping down beside him, Georgina began digging with her hands in the squelching mass. One corner of a picture frame protruded. Working feverishly, tearing their fingers, they dug out a portion of frame with some three-quarters of the painting that she had last seen on the Conte's easel.

'It'll be here,' she sobbed, 'it must be, it has to be.' And oblivious to the mud staining her gown and her bleeding hands she scrabbled away again.

'Let me . . .' Howard began, but she ignored him, caring only that he was working beside her. They found another frame, and in it fragments of the painting that was the duplicate of the other.

'You see,' she exclaimed. 'Please God, he hadn't already sold the Leonardo.'

But they found nothing further, and Georgina turned away despairingly, carrying the paintings and portions of paintings which they had hauled from the mud. And then Howard, following, stumbled.

Turning and glancing towards the jumble of broken bottles, splintered wood and rags that were the residue of the flooding, she saw a half-buried sliver of wood, its gilding glinting in the day's first sunlight.

'Could it . . . ?' She breathed. And together they began tearing at the mud again, thrusting fingers deep into the chill morass, until Howard at last held towards her a frame that was protruding slightly from its protective leather pouch.

'Is — is this . . . ?'

Because the sketch had been left in its frame and covered in leather, although severely stained its lines remained, and she knew she had not drawn them.

'Oh!' she cried, 'oh, thank God.'

She swung round then, clambering the river bank, heedless of Howard's calling after her, unconscious too that her shoes remained in the mud.

Clutching the drawing to her, she was running headlong, unaware of the amazement of passers-by.

At the entrance to the gallery, she hurtled past the liveried man, and then from one room to the next, her dark eyes scanning each in turn for the old familiar features.

The curator smiled at first, then his expression froze. She thrust the picture into the gnarled hands.

'Here,' she said breathlessly. 'I did not steal it. I would not. I wanted only to copy the sketch. Tell me this is the original — almost, I am certain.'

'Child,' the old man said, bleary eyes lighting, 'Do not fret. Alas, I cannot be sure this is the Leonardo, but we'll find those who may . . .'

At the door, Howard halted. Tears coursed down Georgina's cheeks but he alone seemed conscious of them.

'Take me to someone in authority now,' she pleaded.

Howard went with them and his Italian supported Georgina's agitated words as she explained everything to the owner of the gallery.

Someone was hastily despatched to the hospital to charge Vicenzo with theft.

'Other galleries in Florence have lost paintings by means which seem identical,' they were told.

Howard and Georgina exchanged a wry glance.

'Il Conte can paint,' she said. 'Until I arrived he had not thought of faking drawings.'

'We have proof here,' Howard announced,

unloading the mud covered paintings they had recovered on to the desk.

The man nodded. 'I'll wager experts will prove these copies came from the same brush as those left behind elsewhere.'

Her exoneration left Georgina so weak that she leaned heavily upon Howard's arm as they went out into streets drying now under the bright sun.

'I am taking you back to the *castello*,' he told her. 'There you will bathe and change into a fresh gown. We will eat, and then . . .'

'No,' she protested, 'no. My problems may be resolving themselves but you are still at risk.'

'Georgina,' he stated firmly. 'I do not argue.'

'It is for *your* safety,' she insisted. 'So you may escape.'

'And maybe there should be a halt now to my running away,' he said, and beckoned a vacant passing carriage.

They reached the castle over roads newly exposed by the fast draining flood water.

When he heard that none of the female staff were yet returned, Howard assisted Georgina into the bath that Crispino had filled. His touch was gentle as, with soap and sponge, he cosseted away tiredness along with grime.

As Howard wrapped her in a warm towel, a momentary wickedness gleamed in the blue eyes. 'It would be wiser if you were clothed quickly. Otherwise we'll not emerge from here this side of tomorrow! And while you dress and tend to your hair, I'll bathe. And then together, we'll go in search of food.'

Georgina could not feign an appetite. She could do no more than toy with the tempting meats provided by Vicenzo's servant. True, she was free, but where was the joy in that while Howard was so close to being jailed?

'Let us leave Florence,' she begged. 'By some mountain road, so that no one will see us departing.'

'No. I have told you — I must face my enemies. You will remain here while I go into the city.'

'And have some message come that you are taken prisoner?' She shook her head. 'Do you believe that I have forgotten that you stood by me, so short a time ago? Or do you think my loyalty so frail that I'd desert you. You must think me weak if you'll not countenance my coming with you.'

'Weak — you?'

'Then I too go to Florence to face . . . to face those scoundrels who're incapable of judging you aright.'

Though his eyes were troubled, Howard gave a brief smile.

'You wear me down! I'll expend no more fruitless breath!'

As they drove back to Florence he told her he would seek out Roberts at the inn where she'd seen him.

'You will wait in the carriage,' he told her, and received an implacable glare.

She showed him the place where she'd last seen Roberts and, suppressing her fears, she stepped from the *cabriolet*.

Howard went straight to the landlord, asked for Jack Roberts, and was directed to the inn's courtyard.

'Some gentleman enquired for him, signor. But five minutes past.'

They went through to the yard, and halted as their feet touched cobbles. Roberts was there, but sprawling against the horse trough. A finely dressed gentleman was standing over him, his back to them as he dusted himself down with elegant hands.

'Paul . . . ?'

Rushing towards each other, Howard and the man shook hands; Georgina half expected them to embrace, so fervent was their greeting. Pausing only to introduce his friend, Howard led the way back into the inn.

Paul Hardaker was laughing. 'Roberts will have a sore head to keep his mind from our business. And, in any case, he knows now there was no cause to hound you.'

'He does? But what brought you to Florence?'

'Did you think I'd lounge at my desk in York while you were in danger of arrest?'

'But how could you know?'

'That scoundrel out there — he and others like him. Thinking to make a profit out of your misfortune. I read in *The Times* of his claim that he could bring you back to face charges of treason . . . and have you face similar accusations here. I felt certain that the maps you'd prepared for me had aroused such suspicion that men were assuming you a spy.'

'You've not thrown good business away by coming here?'

'On the contrary, I've appointments tomorrow at the vineyard you saw in the Tuscan hills. Business with those in Portugal is already concluded.'

'But the maps I made of Tuscany have disappeared. I've nothing to show you now.'

'The vineyards were abundant were they not, and routes to the sea ports adequate?'

'Both seemed excellent.'

'Then that more than satisfies me. Every

investigation you undertook on my behalf has proved admirable. When all is signed I'll settle our finances. Your share will be handsome, I promise you. And I'll see that Roberts gets his punishment.'

They sat at a table outside a coffee house, within sight of the cathedral and its baptistry. With promises of a celebratory reunion on his return, Paul Hardaker had left them to drive out to the vineyard. Howard sat back into his seat and Georgina sensed the tension draining from him.

'Our problems would seem to be over,' he remarked, staring into the steaming cup as he stirred in sugar. 'We can now concentrate all our efforts on having a relationship to which I, for my part, most certainly look forward. It'll be a fine partnership, Georgina.'

'It is that already, surely?'

'I speak of our marriage.'

'I know.' She lowered her gaze so that he could not see the mischief in her eyes. 'Whilst I refer to the way in which the skill of each of us complements the other.'

'You appear attached to the idea of our working together.'

'I have loved every moment, as I expect to enjoy all our future assignments.'

'You do not see yourself then solely as

mistress of my home, devoting your time entirely to my comforts?'

'Is that how you see me?'

Howard did not answer.

Georgina raised her face and her smile warmed her brown eyes. 'Do you know someone who will better illustrate your books?'

Howard did not answer her. Any who had worked with him had known who was master. Partnership was something new . . .

Slowly, he smiled. It did not hurt, this once, to let her have the last word. There'd be time enough for making a home, for raising a family.

We hope you have enjoyed this Large Print book. Other Thorndike Press or Chivers Press Large Print books are available at your library or directly from the publishers.

For more information about current and upcoming titles, please call or write, without obligation, to:

Thorndike Press
P.O. Box 159
Thorndike, Maine 04986 USA
Tel. (800) 257-5157

OR

Chivers Press Limited
Windsor Bridge Road
Bath BA2 3AX
England
Tel. (0225) 335336

All our Large Print titles are designed for easy reading, and all our books are made to last.